TAILS, CALIFORNIA

A LAKEPORT ROMANCE NOVEL

HEATHER HUFFMAN

Copyright 2021 Heather Huffman

This work is licensed under a Creative Commons Attribution-Noncommercial-No Derivative Works 3.0 Unported License.

Attribution — You must attribute the work in the manner specified by the author or licensor (but not in any way that suggests that they endorse you or your use of the work).

Noncommercial — You may not use this work for commercial purposes.

No Derivative Works — You may not alter, transform, or build upon this work.

Cover Design by James, GoOnWrite.com

Edited by J.C. Wing, Wing Family Editing

This is a work of fiction. Names, characters, places, brands, media, and incidents are either the product of the author's imagination or are used fictitiously. Any resemblance to similarly named places or to persons living or deceased is unintentional.

For Alison, reader and friend, thank you for supporting my work for all of these years—and for making my world bigger and brighter.

CHAPTER 1

*E*ve Bineau blew an errant strand of dark chocolate-colored hair out of her face. She wrapped her arms around her slender frame, the pit of her stomach tightening as she watched the sleek Mercedes drawing nearer. She knew why the landlord was there. It wouldn't be long now until she was handing over the keys to her beloved little knick-knack shop. And then she would have nothing.

Heaven only knew where her vagabond father had landed or what he'd think if he ever made his way back to New Orleans to discover that Eve hadn't had what it took to hang on to Mama's store after her death. Someone with better business sense might have been able to keep the business alive during this last crazy year, but that someone was not Eve.

Of course, someone with better sense at all might have made plans for this moment once they'd seen it coming. Again, that someone was not Eve. She'd been so wrapped up in tying up the loose ends of this life she hadn't even thought about what her next life would look like. Maybe she was more like her free-spirited papa than she preferred to think.

Blinking hard and refusing to give in to the tears that threatened, she watched the little man get out of the big car and saunter her way. Her throat felt like it was closing as she swallowed, willing herself to hold it together as she shook his hand. There weren't many pleasantries to be had on a day like this, so it wasn't long before Eve was taking one last wistful look at the now-empty shop before handing the keys over. She walked away without a backward glance.

Not ready to face her nearly packed apartment, Eve wandered around the streets of her hometown, realizing how utterly apart from it she was. She wandered through the French Marketplace and the Dutch Alley Artist Co-op, wondering how many times she'd walked right past it without even seeing it and how much more was out there in this great big, wide world that she'd never even seen.

She passed some street musicians; they were such a part of the flavor and flair of this city. As she paused to listen to them, something in her felt like they were saying goodbye.

Moving on, Eve's mind turned over her possibilities. She could get a cheaper apartment, but so many of the ones she toured were noisy and two had a rat problem. All of them depressed her. She could try to find a job in another antique store, but she wasn't sure she wanted to spend the rest of her life in the same monotone rhythm she'd spent the first thirty-two years. Her name meant life after all—perhaps she should live hers.

Eve only briefly considered joining the van life movement. She could sink what money she had put back into a van and roam the country until she found the place where she fit. Only the thought of being a woman alone on the road terrified her. She got stressed out trying to figure out where to park her Corolla in a strange place. She couldn't fathom navigating a van.

Tired of meandering around the streets of New Orleans and still not ready to go home, Eve found herself doing what she always did when she needed to clear her head: she drove. She didn't have anywhere in particular to go or see; she just drove, stopping only when she reached the Gulf of Mexico and could go no further.

As Eve pulled the car into a parking place, a line from the radio cut through her fog, "Heads Carolina, tails California...." As the song went on, Eve couldn't help but smile. Maybe the singer had the right idea. Eve had done such a bang-up job with her life choices thus far, perhaps flipping a coin made just as much sense as anything. She fished a quarter out of her repurposed ashtray and flipped it, another smile tugging the corner of her mouth when it came up tails. "Figures," she muttered. "I can't even flip a coin right."

Finding herself somewhere between amused and annoyed, Eve slipped out of the car and began wandering as aimlessly as she'd driven. She found her ambling stopped by the waters of the Gulf once again, so she stood on the Grand Isle pier and watched the horizon as if it would give her some clue as to her next step.

If you were to go to California, a voice in her head asked, *where? It's a big state.*

Behind her, the sound of a child's laughter broke her reverie. She turned to watch the boy's delight as his mom helped him reel in a fish. When they had the poor creature suspended in the air, the boy reached out to grab it, snatching his hand back when the animal began to twist anew.

"Here, I'll do it." A girl Eve could only assume was the boy's older sister reached out to grab the fish, only to snatch her hand back with an "Ouch!" when it got her with its dorsal fin.

"How about you both let me do it?" the mother asked patiently, instructing her daughter to hold the pole while she demonstrated how to take a fish off a hook. Most likely sensing that she was being watched, the mom glanced at Eve and smiled. Eve offered a half-smile in return before averting her gaze, embarrassed to be caught intruding on the family's moment.

I could go someplace where I can teach my children to fish, she decided, still listening to the laughter behind her as she pulled her phone out to Google "fishing in California."

The search engine returned the name of a town, along with popular images. Eve's dark eyes soaked in the pretty turquoise, white, and red buildings in what she could only assume belonged on the town's square. She fell instantly and wholly in love. Just as quickly, she shook it off, chuckling at herself as she dropped the phone in the leg pocket of her cargo capris. *You're being ridiculous*, she mentally admonished before spending the remainder of her trip home trying to put the image of those buildings out of her mind.

Two hours later, Eve was trudging up the steps to her apartment, feeling no closer to an answer.

"Eve! How are you tonight, my dear?" An elderly woman popped her head out of a door, no doubt curious to see who was clomping by.

"Peachy," she lied, forcing a smile. "How are you tonight, Mrs. L?"

"My sciatica is acting up again."

"Try that peppermint oil mix I gave you," Eve reminded her.

"I will, I will. You have a good night, dear."

"You, too."

The conversation only served to depress Eve further. She loved her neighbors, but they were the closest thing she had to friends, and she was the only tenant in this building under seventy. An introverted bookworm through and through, Eve had been all-too-content to limit her human interaction after college to her mother and the people in her immediate vicinity—neighbors and customers. Now, anyone she might have once considered a friend was married with kids and she found herself eating takeout alone each night. She was a couple of cats away from being a cliché, and that terrified her more than the big question mark over her future.

As she warmed up a hodgepodge of leftovers in attempt to empty her fridge, she allowed her mind to wander back to California. She had a decent amount in the bank at the moment, thanks to selling off the inventory at the shop and pretty much everything out of her apartment. She wasn't rolling in money, but she wasn't destitute, either. If ever there was a time in her life when she could do something crazy, Eve supposed it was now.

"I mean, why the hell not?" she demanded out loud, surprising herself. Her dinner forgotten, Eve spent the rest of the night routing a trip she was increasingly bent on making. She had a week left on her lease, but now that the decision had been made, she found it difficult to wait. The next day, she packed her car, cramming full every millimeter of space in her crappy little maroon four-door. With that accomplished, she eyed the car skeptically, thanking God for tow insurance and crossing her fingers she wouldn't need it.

That night, she finished off the last box of cereal for dinner and drank the last swallow of oat milk. She'd sold her TV and packed her books. She'd sold or packed everything except one blanket, her toothbrush, and the clothes on her back. But the books and TV were what she missed most as sleep eluded her that night. At 4 am, she gave up. After one last walk-through of her apartment, she slid the key under the super's door and left her known world behind for an unknown one.

CHAPTER 2

The trip across the country wasn't an easy one, and it left Eve with a much greater appreciation for the women who'd made the trek in a covered wagon, before the age of superhighways and crappy little four-doors.

The first couple hours of the trip were great; the sun was shining, the warm wind felt delicious as it whipped through the tendrils of hair that had escaped her messy bun, and she belted out the musicals piping through her speakers. By the time she reached San Antonio, Texas was wearing thin, and she was sorely tempted to stop and enjoy a nice meal and a stroll down the River Walk.

Every dollar she spent on the road was one less she had to survive on while getting settled, so she pressed on to Fort Stockton. There, she rented the cheapest hopefully-not-gross room she could find before collapsing into bed with only a granola bar for dinner.

The next morning, she rolled out of bed in time for the continental breakfast, where she choked down some sludge they called coffee and inhaled a stale bagel before pushing on. Her energy was renewed when she crossed into New Mexico, putting Texas behind her. Eve felt another burst of energy when she crossed into Arizona, but it was long gone by the time she reached Mesa. Even though it would leave her with an especially long last day on the road, Eve recognized her limitations and found a room for the night in Tonopah.

The next morning rolled around entirely too soon, along with its obscenely long drive and mixed emotions about seeing her destination. Still, she hit the road bright and early. Come nightfall, Eve would have her moment of truth. She'd see her new home without the filter of the internet.

Armed with that knowledge, she twisted her hair into a clip, put on her sunglasses, and cranked the oldies. The trip between Tonopah and LA wasn't especially interesting, but it passed quickly enough. The trip from LA to San Francisco was painful. However frugal Eve might be feeling, she knew she needed to rest before pushing on to her final destination if she hoped to make it alive. By this point in the adventure, she'd driven thirty-two hours in three days. She was so tired her bones hurt and her eyes burned.

Only mildly worried that she was too gnarly to be seen in public, she took a small detour in San Francisco to walk down Pier 39, just to soak up the newness of it all. She grabbed fish and chips from a reliable-looking food truck and ate dinner on a nearby bench. The bustle of people, the din of the infamous Pier 39 sea lions, and the cool breeze that kissed her skin all soothed her frayed nerves. The air was different here. It was at least twenty degrees cooler, and it didn't cling to you like it did back home. She took a deep breath, wondering if it was this temperate in her new home.

Eve stretched her screaming muscles one more time before getting up to meander back to her car. It was time to find out what her new world was like. By the time she made it out of the city traffic and north to the little town nestled on Clear Lake, it was dusk, and her eyes were so heavy she had to smack herself every few minutes to keep them propped open. She debated pulling to the side of the road to rest for just ten minutes but didn't trust herself not to fall truly and deeply asleep, leaving herself vulnerable to pretty much anything. Her GPS gave her about point-two second's notice before telling her to hang a left. She went to comply, slamming on her brakes when her brain registered the man crossing the street.

"Watch where you're going!" he bellowed.

Eve blinked back tired tears. She wasn't the type for public outbursts, but she found herself shouting back that he was a jerk. Her hands were still shaking when she pulled into the parking lot of the little inn she'd chosen for her stay, The Shattered Kelpie, which stood adjacent to a pub called The Mortal Kelpie. She'd chosen it because the name amused her. She hadn't the faintest idea what it meant, but it was quirky and fun. She could only hope the place lived up to the promise its moniker held.

After resting her head on the steering wheel for a moment to collect her nerves, Eve propelled herself out of the car and through the door. Her excitement over having arrived at her destination was tempered by the empty room that greeted her. She waited a couple of moments before wondering if the place was closed. A few more moments and she began debating if she should try somewhere else. It was a tourist town; she could throw a rock and hit another inn if she wanted.

Just as she resolved to try her luck elsewhere, a woman burst into the room amidst a flurry of breathless apologies. Eve was startled by the clarity of the other woman's apple-green eyes. Her rust-colored hair spilled out of its ties and down her back. A smattering of freckles dusted her button nose. Eve wanted to be irritated with the woman but found herself inexplicably pulled to like her.

"I'm so sorry," she said for the fifth time. "We just had a rush next door and our desk clerk called out tonight, so I'm running back and forth between the two."

"I didn't mean to trouble you—" Eve hesitated, wondering if she should leave.

"Nonsense. No trouble at all." The woman waved her off.

"It's settled down now and reinforcements have arrived. What can I do for you, my dear?"

"I was hoping you might have a room available?"

"Good thing you came this week instead of next." The redhead nodded. "I'm sure we can round something up for you for a couple of days, but we're booked solid starting next Thursday."

Eve nodded in return. "Okay. Good to know."

The other woman eyed her for a second before extending a hand. "I'm Corinne. My brothers and I own the Kelpies."

"I'm Eve." Any further explanation was cut off by the fact that Eve had no clue what she could possibly say about herself that wouldn't sound absolutely insane.

"Well Eve, it's nice to meet you. If I can get your driver's license and a credit card, we'll see about getting you a room for the night."

"Thanks." She handed over the requested cards and resisted the urge to melt against the counter in exhaustion.

Corinne whistled. "You're from New Orleans, huh? I've always wanted to go there."

"You should. It's pretty cool."

"If you don't mind me asking, what's a flight in from there cost?"

"I don't know. I drove."

"You drove?" Corinne choked on disbelief.

"I don't recommend it," Eve admitted.

"How long of a drive is that?"

"Thirty-four hours, plus bathroom breaks." Eve felt the tired weigh even more heavily now that she'd said the words aloud.

"I hope you're staying long enough to recover from a trip like that."

"Me, too." She signed the piece of paper Corinne handed her, sliding it back before scooping up her credit card and license.

"Your room is just down that hall." Corinne pointed before handing Eve her keycard. "It's probably easiest to just come back through these front doors. Do you have many bags? I'll get someone to carry them for you."

"That's okay." Eve tried to protest but Corinne waved her off again. She got the impression the woman did that a lot.

"Nonsense. You look exhausted. We'll let one of my big, strapping brothers do it. Having the lugs around should be good for something."

"I don't need much just for tonight. I'll be right back." Eve left to retrieve her bag, cursing under her breath when the car didn't want to easily relinquish its hold on the mammoth suitcase that had most likely seen its prime in 1984. She backed through the door, pausing long enough to wrestle the suitcase through those doors as well.

Behind her, she could hear a male voice talking to Corinne. "I tell you, the crazies are out in full force tonight. One of them nearly mowed me down on my way here."

"You are such a drama queen," Corinne retorted.

Eve stopped cold. *It couldn't be.* She turned, wishing with all her might it was a different pedestrian who'd nearly been mowed down by a different crazy. *Damn.* It was her pedestrian, and she was the crazy.

"Hello again." She waved feebly.

"Come to finish the job, huh?" His eyes narrowed.

"Don't tempt me," Eve tossed back before she realized what she was doing.

"Oh, so you've met Callum," Corinne stated simply.

"I'm sorry." Eve reigned in her temper. "I just didn't see you. I was tired and my GPS was being a jerk."

Corinne's grin deepened. "That's okay, Eve. People who've known him for years try to kill him on a regular basis."

"Very funny." Callum's scowl deepened in direct contrast with his sister's amused expression.

"Was it?"

Eve shifted the weight of the bag from one hand to the other, unsure what to do next.

Corinne smacked her brother on the back of the head. "Get her bag, you dunderhead."

"Don't push it," he growled.

Corinne put a hand on her hip.

Callum sighed and went to do as he had been told.

"It's okay. You don't have to—" Eve resisted his tug on the handle of her bag.

"Forget it. I'll never hear the end of it if I don't." He tugged again, this time she released her hold.

"Well then. Who am I to stand in the way of a grown man afraid of his sister?"

Corinne snickered. Callum's frown was fierce.

"And here I thought chivalry was dead." Eve couldn't help getting in one more jab as she fell in step behind him.

"Good night, Eve," Corinne called after her.

"Good night, Corinne," Eve called down the hall.

Callum huffed. It was a sound that made Eve think of an irritated bear. She bit the inside of her cheek to keep from smiling. He came to a stop in front of a door that she figured to be hers. It took half a second for her to remember she had the key, so she reached around him to unlock the door.

Wowza, he smells fantastic. No matter how irritating he was, Eve had to admit that much. The errant thought caused her to fumble with the lock just long enough for him to reach around her to help.

"There's a bit of a trick to it," he explained, glancing over at her.

He was close. Too close. She didn't remember the last time she'd been in a man's arms, which had been the ultimate effect of all the reaching around they'd done to master the lock. He twisted the handle and pushed the door open; she tumbled through it like a skittish animal breaking free of its captor.

"I'm stupidly tired," she offered by way of explanation, feeling like a clueless fool.

His head dipped in acknowledgment. Or amusement. She

couldn't be sure which. "Then get some sleep. Tomorrow's a new day, and I don't know if our little town can handle too much excitement."

And then she was alone in her room. After walking around for a moment to take stock of the place, she made her way to the window, hoping to see something of the town. All she could really see was the parking lot, though she suspected the bobbing lights on the horizon were boats on the lake.

Eve grabbed a shower, letting the water wash away the grime of the day and the soreness in her muscles. As she towel-dried her hair, she looked longingly at the bed, tempted to crawl in and allow oblivion to claim her. But as exhausted as she might be, she was equally curious. The muffled sounds of the adjoining pub beckoned her. *Just one drink*, she reasoned with herself. *Just to see what it's like.*

Eve braided her wet hair and slid on a peasant skirt and tank top, not bothering with makeup. After sliding on sandals and triple checking that she had her key and wallet, she padded down the hall in search of the pub.

She found it with relative ease, taking in the decor as she made her way to the bar. The wood and exposed brick interior made her think of a real Scottish tavern, or what she imagined one would look like, anyway.

"You must be Eve," a cheerful man greeted her from behind the bar even as a happy yellow dog padded up to give her a friendly sniff. She held her hand out to the animal before scratching behind its ear.

The man looked so much like Callum that she did a second take. "You're too cheerful to be Callum. Are you Corinne's other brother?"

The man guffawed before offering his hand. "Ian, at your service. And that's Sadie. You can shoo her away if she's bothering you." He nodded in the direction of the dog.

"It's nice to meet you, Ian and Sadie. How did you know who I am?"

"My sister said an exotic beauty checked in tonight. Either there's a surplus of those, or she was talking about you."

Eve felt her cheeks heating up. "I think that's the nicest thing anybody has said to me ever."

"Then you're hanging around with the wrong people." He patted her hand before letting it go. "Now. What can I get you?"

"I don't know." Eve found her brain to be incapable of making even the simplest of decisions. "Surprise me. Something Californian."

"How do you feel about vermouth?"

She eyed him skeptically.

"No really. This vermouth isn't what you think. Try this." He mixed a drink and pushed it her direction, watching her expectantly.

She held the glass to her lips, flicking her tongue against the rim before taking a sip. "Oh. Wow. That is good."

Ian grinned at her. "We're having a bit of a vermouth revolution here in Northern California."

"Who knew?" She took another sip. The drink might not become her go-to, but it wasn't bad, and it was different. This adventure was all about different. "What is this?"

"Sutton and Soda."

"Thank you." She took another drink, the warmth of the liquor beginning to spread through her. The dog had placed itself at her feet and was now looking up at her expectantly. Eve patted its head again.

Ian moved away from her, pulling dirty glasses off the bar and putting them in a dish tub before returning to wipe the counter down. "So, why California?"

"Because California won the coin toss." She shrugged.

"Excuse me?" He stopped what he was doing and turned to give her his undivided attention.

Maybe what they say about bartenders is true, and they're just easy to talk to. Or maybe it was the vermouth. Or maybe she just desperately needed to tell another living soul what she'd done. Whatever the reason, the words tumbled out, slowly at first but gaining momentum as the story unfolded.

By the time she was sucking the ice cubes in what had been her drink, she'd told him everything. This stranger knew she'd moved halfway across the country on a coin toss and a good measure of desperation for something new, something different. He knew she had no job and nowhere to sleep as of Thursday once their hotel was booked solid.

"Well, my friend, you have moxie. I'll say that much for you."

"I'll tell myself that's a good thing." She sighed and slid off her barstool, tightening her grip on the rail long enough to make sure both feet were squarely under her. She was so tired she couldn't see straight; maybe going out hadn't been her best decision ever. But she'd made a friend, and that was something.

"It is a good thing." Ian's smile was genuine and wholly enchanting. Eve smiled back at him as the two parted ways. That night, as she laid in her bed, relishing the feel of the sheets on her toes, the last thought to flit through her brain was to wonder if Callum ever smiled like that.

CHAPTER 3

*E*ve slowly came to the realization that the pounding wasn't part of a dream or a repercussion from her lone drink the night before, but rather a persistent knocking at her door. She rolled out of bed, stumbling a bit when her legs refused to work properly. She opened the door without checking, briefly hoping she wouldn't find a murderer on the other side of the threshold.

Thankfully, it wasn't a murderer. She was greeted by Corinne's smiling face. The woman held a cup out to Eve. "I brought you a café au lait."

"Really?" Eve peeked at the pale liquid.

"Well, something like it. It was the only New Orleans drink I could think of, besides a hurricane, and it's probably a bit early for that."

Eve shrugged, taking a sip of the coffee. It was awful. "It's delightful. Thank you so much."

"Really?" Corinne brightened.

"Yeah, really," Eve lied. Corinne showing up on her doorstep at the crack of dawn with a gift was just about the sweetest thing ever, and that's all that mattered.

"What sounds good for breakfast—the café or the bakery?"

"Which is more likely to have hash browns?"

"The café," Corinne answered.

"Then that gets my vote," Eve answered without thinking. "Wait, why?"

"Because we're going to breakfast, silly." Corinne said it with such assurance, Eve knew it would be pointless to argue.

"Ah. Good to know."

"Get dressed," she ordered. "I'll meet you in the lobby in an hour."

Once Eve was alone, it occurred to her that an hour was more than she needed; she could sleep for half of that and still have plenty of time to get ready.

She could not, however, sleep for fifty-five minutes and still get ready. Unfortunately, she'd dozed for longer than intended, leaving Eve to get dressed faster than she ever had in her life, shimmying into the closest thing she could grab, which was the same outfit she'd worn to the tavern the night before, before letting her hair out of the braid she'd slept in and running her fingers through it in lieu of a brush. She settled for lip gloss and a quick sweep of mascara. There was no time for more.

Not even looking in the mirror, lest it tell her she was crazy to be seen in public, she snagged her wallet and phone off the dresser and darted out the door. As soon as she heard the latch click shut behind her, she closed her eyes and swore. The key was still on the dresser. She tested the handle, just in case, before relegating that to being a problem for later and scurrying down the hall to meet her newfound friend.

Corinne looked up from the conversation she was having with the front desk clerk; her face brightening when she saw Eve. "Yay, you're here!"

"In the flesh." Eve gave a little curtsey, feeling silly as soon as she did. She was blaming lack of sleep, but Corinne didn't seem to notice. She rounded the corner, snagged Eve's hand, and led her out the door. Being led along wasn't entirely bad. It freed Eve up to soak in her surroundings. The little hamlet was every bit as darling as she'd hoped. Only now that it was real instead of virtual, she could inhale the cool, fresh air. There was a breeze that hinted of fall. Eve's skin responded, goosebumps appearing on her arms.

"Is it always this chilly in August?" Eve wrapped her arms around herself, wishing she'd grabbed an over-shirt.

"I wouldn't exactly call this chilly, but it is a little early for summer and fall to start playing tug-of-war," Corinne admitted.

"Where I'm from, you can cut the air with a knife in August."

"Did you like it? New Orleans, I mean."

Eve paused in thought. "Yeah. I did. Well enough, anyway."

Corinne opened the door for Eve, ushering her inside a café straight out of another era. The waitress waved at them as Corinne led the way to a corner table. "I like this one," she explained, sliding into her seat. "So. If you liked New Orleans well enough, why leave?"

Eve raised a shoulder in a half shrug, staring at the menu without seeing. She wasn't sure what she could say that wouldn't sound insane. The waitress saved her from having to respond by appearing to take their order. She ordered hash browns and coffee and waited for Corinne to finish her order.

"... and go ahead and give me sausage with those pancakes. And some hash browns."

"Alright, I'll get that order put in for you." The waitress went to pocket her ticket book when Corinne held up her hand.

"You know what, Anna? Can you bring us one of those homemade donuts of yours while we wait?"

Eve arched an eyebrow, impressed.

"I'm hormonal," she offered by way of explanation. "And you were about to tell me why you left New Orleans."

"I was?"

"Were you on the run from the law?"

A smile tugged the corner of Eve's mouth. "No, nothing like that."

"An abusive ex?"

Eve shook her head.

"Are you that woman that tripped into the fountain because you were texting? If so, then you're internet famous now. You should capitalize on that."

"No internet fame for me." Eve's tone was almost apologetic. "I just didn't have anything tying me there. When my business went under, and I didn't know what was next, I flipped a coin. California won."

"So, you flipped a coin, packed your things, and moved," Corinne recapped.

"Pretty much."

"Wow. I didn't believe Ian when he told me."

"Isn't there some kind of bartender/customer confidentiality thing?"

Corinne shook her head. "I don't think that's a thing."

"I'm pretty sure it is," Eve argued.

"I'm pretty sure it's not."

"You might want to double check. I mean, the scandal could rock the bartending industry if you're wrong."

"I'll add it to my to-do list." Corinne laughed. "So, you really just packed up and headed to California?"

Eve held her hands up as if to say *ta-da*. "I really did."

"I don't know that I could have done that. This town, it's always been my world. My brothers, as crazy as they make me, I can't imagine life without them. Holy cow, you should have seen the drama when Mama and Pop decided to sell their shares in the Kelpies so they could travel."

"That's amazing." Eve eyed the donut being set in the middle of their table.

"Having roots, or that donut?"

"Both," Eve admitted. "Is that an actual donut?"

"Gourmet, baby."

"Oh my heavens; I'm in love." The warm, flaky delicacy melted on her tongue, a delectable medley of flavor. Eve closed her eyes to savor the experience.

"Yeah. They're unreal."

"Admit it. You don't stay here for your brothers. You're here for the donuts."

"Maybe a little," Corinne admitted.

"A girl's got to have priorities." Eve enjoyed the easy camaraderie she felt with Corinne. For some reason, the woman made her forget to be shy. "It's nice of you, coming to breakfast with me, showing me around."

"I'm just happy to have another woman close to my age around."

"Is there a shortage of us?"

"It's a small town." Corinne paused. "Or maybe I just don't get out much. The Kelpies keep me pretty busy."

"My store kept me pretty busy back in New Orleans. And I think I was a bit of a recluse. Anyway, I decided it was time to start living my life instead of reading about other people's."

"What kind of store was it?"

"Knick-knacks and stuff. Antiques."

"Did you like it, having your own place?"

"I loved the antiques—finding treasures, wondering what stories they had to tell, helping people find the perfect piece for their home. But I was terrible with the money part. Rent kept going up and I just couldn't bring myself to raise prices fast enough to keep up. So, I wasn't a fan of being the boss, no."

Corinne's eyes brightened. "Good, because I have a brilliant idea."

"Are you going to share your brilliant idea with me?" Eve prompted.

"Later. After breakfast."

Eve let it drop, but she couldn't help spending the rest of their meal wondering what Corinne was up to. When the women were finished eating, they argued briefly over who would cover the check. Corinne won the argument. Eve had the impression Corinne won most arguments.

They left the diner, ambling down the sidewalk to the heart

of old town. Eve was absolutely in love with the rows of brightly painted buildings—turquoise, red, white—all neatly coordinated to create an enchanting effect. Eve wanted to wander through all of the stores, to see what treasures each held. But Corinne seemed to be a woman on a mission, so she didn't ask about stopping; she just made a mental note to return later on her own. The pair came to a stop in front of a pale green building with the words Dragonfly Antiques scrawled above the door in white cursive. Corinne pulled open the door and motioned with her head for Eve to enter.

Eve's shop in New Orleans, like so many of the antique stores dotting Royal Street, had been dark and cluttered. This store was bright and cheerful. Still a bit cluttered, as was the nature of any antique store, but it was pristine compared to what she was used to.

"I'll be right back if you want to have a look around," Corinne said.

"Sure thing." Eve was happy to be left to her own devices for a bit. She could easily spend hours exploring this place. She was a bit dismayed when Corinne returned a mere minutes later, arm in arm with a stunning redhead. The woman was probably fifty, though Eve was terrible at guessing ages. She had gorgeous auburn hair and the brightest blue eyes Eve had ever seen.

"Eve, this is Moira. She owns the Dragonfly. Moira, this is Eve, the friend I was telling you about."

"Nice to meet you."

"You too, Eve." Moira took her by surprise with a handshake. The woman's hand was warm, her grip somehow light without feeling weak. Eve had the distinct impression she was being sized up. "Corinne tells me you just moved to town, and that you used to own a shop like mine."

"I don't think mine was quite as nice as this, but I did."

"It just so happens that I've been looking to hire someone to help manage this place, but not many young people are interested in spending their days with antiques. I don't suppose you would be?"

"Very much." Eve hoped she didn't look overly eager.

"Good." Moira's lips hinted at a smile. "I'll get an application for you to fill out. But Corinne here recommends you so highly, I think we can at least give it a try."

"That would be wonderful. Thank you, Moira." Eve followed the woman to the register, where Moira fished under the counter for a moment before producing the promised application.

"Fill this out and bring it back and we can talk particulars."

Eve left the store on cloud nine. "I could hug you, Corinne. Thank you so much."

"I didn't want to say anything just in case the spot had been filled. But Moira's just the best. You'll love working there."

"I don't have the job yet." Eve was reminding herself as much as Corinne.

"Oh, I'm sure it's yours if you want it. Moira is tired of being tied down. She has one employee, but Lily's still in high school and can only work part-time. Moira's been saying for a year that she wants to hire a full-time manager so she can take a step back someday."

"I've never thought much about fate, but I'm beginning to wonder."

"Yeah, I never realized a coin toss could be such a solid way to make a decision, but it seems to be working for you."

Eve hoped that was the case. As the two women parted ways, she returned to her room, only to remember she'd locked herself out. *Damn it.* She sighed and went back to the front desk. To her dismay, it wasn't Corinne the clerk called up to help but Callum.

"I should have known it was you." Callum barely cast a glance her way before heading down the hall to her room.

Was he laughing at her? Eve was pretty sure he was.

"There ya go." He opened the door and stood back for her to pass.

"Thank you." Eve rose her chin a notch, determined to look

as regal as possible as she moved past him. That determination was thwarted when she caught her toe on something and lurched forward. His arm shot out, catching her around the waist before she face-planted on the carpet. She closed her eyes, her face burning with mortification as he easily set her upright again.

"You okay?"

"Mentally or physically?" She dropped her head, resting it on him without even meaning to.

"Um, both?"

Eve realized his arm was still around her waist and her forehead was resting on this total stranger's shoulder. What on earth was wrong with her? She took a step back, forcing herself to look him in the eye. "I'll let you know if I figure it out. Thanks for catching me."

"Anytime." The corner of his lip twitched.

Okay, now she was sure he was laughing at her. What sane human wouldn't be? A kind person would leave quickly to allow her to be alone in her abject horror. He lingered, confirming her suspicion that he was not a nice man. Still, she couldn't help meeting his bright blue gaze. Was he looking for something or was this just a random staring contest? Eve couldn't be certain. Just like that, he broke the connection, striding off before she could figure out what was going on.

Alone in her room, Eve grabbed a shirt to wear over her tank top. The sun had warmed the air outside, but it was still much cooler than she was used to. She grabbed her key, lest she forget it a second time, and then sat down to fill out the application she was still clutching. It was a little wrinkled and worse for the wear, but there was nothing she could do about that now.

There wasn't much to fill out—she hadn't gone to school beyond her associate degree, and the only place she'd ever worked was her parents' antique store, which she'd inherited when her mother died. For references, she led off with Corinne, leaving the "years known" section blank. Other than that, she had only a favorite professor and a distant cousin to list. Sure, she knew other people, but they were acquaintances, Facebook friends at best.

The more depressed the application made her, the surlier she got. As her mood descended, her irritation with Callum climbed. Eve knew that if she were being rational, she'd see that she wasn't mad at Callum so much as simply mad, but that thought just pissed her off even more.

She finished the application and checked for the key one more time before heading back to the Dragonfly. Eve breathed a sigh of relief when she didn't bump into Callum in the lobby. The sigh turned to a swear word when she noticed him unloading a case of beer from the back of his Jeep.

"Hey Eve, do you know about how long you'll be?"

"No clue, why?"

"Just wanted to be sure I was here to let you back in your room when you got back."

Eve couldn't think of a reply that was appropriate to shout across the parking lot, so she merely held up her room key in response. Callum's laughter followed her down the sidewalk. She fumed the entire way there, pausing outside of the Dragonfly long enough to straighten her shoulders and will the scowl off her face.

"Eve." Moira brightened when she recognized her. "I'm glad to see you back already."

"I'm eager to find a job," she admitted. "And a place, but first things first."

"You're looking for a place, too?"

"Yeah. I'm at the Kelpie until Thursday, but after that is a bit of a question mark."

"You know, there's a studio apartment above the Dragonfly." Moira pointed up. "It's a mess, but if you want to clean it up, you can have it cheap."

"Really?" It was Eve's turn to brighten.

"Sure. I'd sleep better at night knowing someone was keeping an eye on the store."

"That would be amazing."

"Do you want to at least see it first?"

As much as Eve thought she'd been happy with anything that wasn't a cardboard box right now, she probably should at least take a look at the place. "I'd love to see it."

Moira nodded once, pulling a set of keys out from the cash register. "I'll let you in, then we can chat after you've had a chance to check it out."

Eve followed Moira up the narrow steps, musing to herself that if she did take the apartment, she'd need small furniture unless she planned to teleport it. Moira fought with the lock for a moment before the door swung open. Eve couldn't help thinking that would probably amuse Callum. Thoughts of the troublesome Scot skittered away the moment Eve stood in the apartment alone. She turned a slow circle, the dirt and dust fading away in her mind's eye.

Moira had been right, the place was a mess. But it had potential. Other than the bathroom, it was one large room, but the building had enough nooks and crannies to provide natural divisions. The walls were a mixture of brick, beadboard, and massive windows. The wall facing the town square offered a built-in bench and windows that blended into a sharply angled skylight. Eve couldn't wait to curl up there to read on a rainy day.

There was a daunting amount of work to be done, but with a good scrubbing, a coat of paint, and some rugs, it could be an amazing little apartment. Eve knew if she lingered, she'd get her hopes up beyond all repair, so she scurried back to find Moira in the store.

"It's too cute for words," Eve announced her presence.

"You like it?" Moira looked up from her work.

"It's perfect, but I'm almost afraid to ask what you want for it."

"I'm sure we can work something out if you're willing to do

the cleaning. I like the idea of having someone I trust living above the store."

Eve wanted to ask why Moira was willing to trust her, but she didn't want to plant a seed of doubt. Instead, she turned the discussion back to her most pressing issue. "So, does that mean I have the job?"

Moira smiled. "Yes, it's yours if you want it."

The two women spent the next half hour working out the details. The pay wasn't great, but it was reasonable with a raise in ninety days. The rent was more than her apartment in New Orleans had been, but less than she'd expected in California. All in all, Eve couldn't believe her luck in having met Corinne. When she said as much, Moira smiled again. "Those McTavish kids are something special."

"Two of them are, anyway," Eve muttered before thinking.

The other woman laughed outright. "I see my nephew already impressed you with his bullheadedness. He has a knack for that."

Eve paled. "I'm an idiot. I'm so sorry. I shouldn't have said that."

Moira waved her off and Eve knew where Corinne had picked up the gesture. "Nonsense. Callum is a delightful young man, but I know him well enough to know sometimes you have to get through a few rough outer layers to see it."

"I'll take your word for it." Eve didn't buy it for one second.

"He'll grow on you," Moira predicted, putting the subject to rest.

CHAPTER 4

*E*ve was fairly certain she had more white paint on herself than the walls. She put the roller back on the tray and stepped back to assess her handiwork. She'd debated a dozen different colors for the walls before settling on just plain old white. It seemed fitting with the old boards; it made them look fresh and clean again. Of course, she'd also scrubbed the entire place top to bottom—her hands would probably smell like bleach well into the next decade.

She moved out of the inn tomorrow. In three short days, she'd performed nothing short of a miracle on the little apartment in her free time before and after her shifts at the store. She might not have furniture yet, but the place was immaculate, the walls were painted, and she'd hung some darling little dragonfly lights. And she had a fluffy rug that felt amazing on her bare toes. A girl didn't need a whole lot more than that, by Eve's way of thinking.

That is, until she went downstairs, intent on heading over to the Kelpie for lunch with Corinne and stopped short at the weathered turquoise bookcase that had been added to the store's inventory sometime during the morning.

"Moira, what do you want for this one?" Eve bent over to

inspect the furniture more closely. It was good, solid wood. Whoever refinished it had done an excellent job. She ran her hands along the wood, marveling at how soft it felt. Her finger traced the scrollwork almost lovingly.

"It's darling, isn't it?"

"It really is. I know exactly where I'd put it, too."

"You know we have an employee discount, right?"

"Oh, that's a very dangerous thing." Eve bit her lip. "But I think I need this. Not want, need."

Moira patted her hand. "I'll get Callum to lug it upstairs for you."

"Oh no. I don't want to bother him."

"Nonsense. He's just finishing unloading the rest. He won't mind."

Moira had been wrong. Callum minded, as evidenced by the scowl that settled over his face when his aunt asked him to move the bookcase once more.

"I just set it down. Where does it need to go now?"

"Upstairs. Eve bought it."

"Ah." If he had more to say on the subject, he didn't.

Eve mentally filled in the blanks. *Of course, it's Eve making me wrestle the stupid thing up a narrow staircase. Maybe she wants to load it down with books first….*

He had the bookcase strapped to a dolly and was backing toward the stairs by the time Eve thought to go with him so she could open the door.

With every step he maneuvered, she found herself wondering if she should help or stay out of the way. "I feel pretty useless," she admitted.

"It's okay; I got it." The strain was evident in his voice.

"No, here, let me help." Eve bent over, grabbing the lip of the dolly by either side, hoisting it up the step. Callum hadn't accounted for the extra boost and somehow his feet got in the way.

He let out a string of expletives. "Are you absolutely positive you aren't trying to kill me?"

Eve had intended to apologize, but his anger seemed disproportionate, and it stirred her own. "Don't be such a baby. Your toe will live."

"Great. Thank you for the diagnosis."

"Anytime." Eve resisted the urge to help again. They finally reached her landing, where he waited for her to shimmy past to open the door. Naturally, the door was completely uninclined to open for her. "It does this for Moira, too."

"Uh-huh."

"No, for real. It wouldn't open for her the first time she showed me the place."

He held up his hands as if to say he wasn't going to argue with her, but everything in his face said he was highly amused by her inability to open doors.

The lock finally succumbed to her finagling or to the threats she was leveling at it, either one. "There, see?" she felt victorious as the door swung open.

"Very good. You opened a door." He wheeled the bookcase through the opening. "Where do you want this?"

"I'm not sure you want to know where I'd like to stick that bookcase right now."

Callum stopped, raising an eyebrow in response.

"That wall will suffice." She pointed, following him over to run her fingers along the wood one more time after the piece was in place. "It's lovely."

"Thank you."

"I meant the bookcase."

"I know, although I'm flattered you think that statement could somehow apply to me, too. But I refinished it."

"You did this?"

"Does that ruin it for you? Because I really don't want to take that thing back down the steps."

"I'll overlook it. Nothing's perfect." The sass in her voice surprised her. Eve had to admit she enjoyed bickering with this man.

"That's big of you." He finished wrapping the straps around the dolly and headed toward the door.

"I thought so. Thank you for helping get the bookcase up here."

"Helping?"

"You know you couldn't have done it without that boost I gave you." Eve amused herself.

"You mean when you set the case on my toe? If I lose my toenail, you'll be hearing from me."

"The entire town will hear you whining if you lose a toenail."

He paused on her landing, surveying her. "You're not exactly sugar and spice, are you sweetheart?"

"Maybe a little more spice than sugar," she admitted.

"Just a bit."

She could see the laughter dancing in his eyes, her irritation wicking away in response. "I'll be sure to apologize to your sister for you."

"And why should I apologize to my sister?"

"For making me late to lunch."

"I made you late for lunch?" He folded his arms across his chest and leaned against the wall.

"Yeah. It was kind of rude, actually."

He pushed himself away from the wall. "In that case, I'd better deliver you and my apologies right away. Maybe I'll even offer to stay and buy her lunch, just to be safe."

She hadn't seen that one coming. "You own the restaurant. I don't think that counts as buying lunch."

"It's worth a shot. Come on, I'll give you a ride down."

Eve would have argued, but she truly was late, and it seemed a bit silly to when he was parked right out front, and they were headed in the same direction. "Sure, thanks."

She couldn't be certain, but Eve got the impression he was surprised by how quickly she agreed. "Don't forget your key."

Eve's brain failed to supply a retort, so she rolled her eyes at him. She was going to have to brush up on her witty banter if she was going to keep up with Callum.

"So, when's the rest of your furniture getting in?" he asked conversationally after they were en route to the Kelpie.

"It's not."

"It's not?"

"I sold it to pay for the trip. Or help pay for it, anyway," she explained.

"So, you don't have any furniture?"

"I have some boxes. Mostly books and clothes. A few mementos. Oh, and my elephant lamp."

"Well, as long as the elephant lamp made the cut."

Eve folded her arms across her chest. "Hey now. That is a super cute lamp. Don't judge me."

"So, you have a fully stocked bookcase, your clothes, an elephant lamp, and that is the extent of your possessions?"

Eve took mental inventory. "Yep. Pretty much."

"I think you and I have very different priorities."

"Oh, wait. I forgot—I brought my wine rack."

"Priorities," he repeated.

"Exactly."

His chuckle was rich and deep, filling Eve with warmth. She smiled, looking out the window lest he sense the shyness that washed over her.

"It's such a pretty little town. Like something out of a movie."

"Yeah, I guess it is. I don't know that I've ever really noticed."

"It's easy to overlook everyday beauty," she mused. Silence settled over the car. Eve couldn't be sure if he was contemplating her words or the fact that she had a unique ability to kill conversations. It was her superpower.

Whether it was due to her superpower or his schedule, Callum didn't make good on his threat to accompany her and

Corinne to lunch. He dropped her in front of the tavern with a cheerful goodbye.

"Was that my brother's Jeep you just got out of?" Corinne asked by way of hello, her tone hinting at hope.

"He was dropping some furniture off at the Dragonfly and offered to give me a ride since I was running late," Eve explained, hoping to put her friend's suspicions to rest.

"Is your car okay?"

"Yeah, it's fine. He said he was headed this way anyway, though."

"Then why did he just pull out in the opposite direction?"

Corinne had her there. Eve tucked the information away to puzzle over later. "I'm famished." Her stomach obligingly growled to back up her story.

"All right." Corinne relented, leading her to a back booth. "I'll let you off the hook for now."

"Eve!" Ian greeted her brightly as he emerged from the backroom with Sadie on his heels. As soon as the dog saw the women, she made a beeline over for attention. Eve had never been much of a pet person, but Sadie made a good argument for dogs. There was something endearing about the adoration in her eyes.

"Hey, Ian!" She returned his cheerful greeting. "What's good today?"

He held his hand to his chest as if protecting his heart. "I'm wounded you would ask that. All of it's good every day, my dear."

"Let me rephrase—what's *especially* good today?"

"Better." He paused. "I say go with the fish and chips."

"Sounds perfect. Gimme one of those and can I have one of those frozen lemonade things?"

"I'll have the same," Corinne chimed in, then turned her attention to Eve. "How the hell do you stay so tiny eating like that?"

"You just ordered the same thing."

"Yeah, but I'll spend an hour at the gym tonight trying to work it off. You're going to curl up in your reading nook. It's nowhere even close to fair."

Eve wasn't sure what to say to that. The best she could offer was a small shrug before changing the subject. "So, is the fish local?"

"Definitely not." Corinne shook her head for emphasis. "The mercury content in the lake is too high for the fish to be edible."

"So, it's the fishing capital of the state, but you can't eat the fish? That's a bummer."

It was Corinne's turn to shrug. "Who knows? Maybe the catch and release program is why there's such good fishing to begin with."

"Always looking on the bright side of things."

"Speaking of happy things...," Corinne leaned in conspiratorially. "I wonder why Callum said he was coming this way. I think he just wanted to get you in his car."

"I highly doubt that. But it is weird, he said he wanted to come to lunch and then just left. You might not have noticed this, but your brother is a strange man."

Corinne briefly pursed her lips. "Not usually. I think you make him do strange things."

"I think you're imagining things."

"Okay." Corinne let it drop, but the smile playing on her lips said she wasn't sold. "I'm going to go get our lemonades since my other brother seems to have disappeared, too."

Eve nodded, her mind wandering to what on earth had gotten into Callum McTavish. It hadn't gone far when Corinne was back, setting their drinks on the table before sliding back into her seat.

"So, how's work going?"

Eve was almost suspicious at how quickly Corinne changed the conversation but chose to simply be grateful instead. "Work's not bad. No, actually, it's great. It probably sounds crazy, but I love cleaning and organizing all of the furniture and knick-knacks, getting to know each piece and wondering what its story is."

"Moira says she's had a banner week so far, so I know she's happy."

Eve took a drink of her lemonade slush, pinching the bridge of her nose when she gave herself an ice cream headache. "I think people are just coming to check out the new girl."

"Yeah, we get a lot of tourists but not many transplants. People are curious."

"You know what I'm curious about?"

"What's that?" Corinne asked.

"Why do they call Crazy Molly crazy? She seems so nice."

Corinne caught herself off guard with her own laugh and choked on her lemonade. It took her a minute to answer the question. "She used to be just Molly. The crazy part was added when she backed over her husband, Bill. On purpose. Lucky for her, he lived."

Eve considered for a moment. "What did Bill do?"

"In response or to deserve being run over by a Dodge Ram truck?"

"Both, I guess."

"He didn't retaliate. I think he was too scared. As for deserving it, he kind of did. She caught him cheating. I mean, he cheated on her pretty much since the day after their wedding, and I think she always suspected as much, but catching him in the act pushed her over the edge. The whole town could hear her ranting, 'You think I'm crazy? I'll show you crazy.' She backed right over the poor bastard."

"Good for her."

"I'll be sure to warn Callum not to get a wandering eye."

"I knew you hadn't let that go."

Corinne giggled. "I don't know. She could have just left him, moved on with her life and then he'd be forever known as Two-Timing Bill. But instead, she's stuck with Crazy Molly and few people stop to ask why she did it."

"True, but I had a boyfriend who pulled that crap. I'd be sure he was up to something, he'd tell me I was crazy, and so the cycle went until I caught him in the act. Knowing someone intentionally made you feel crazy to cover their own sleazy actions, that stirs up a special kind of wrath. Yeah, I think Molly and I will be friends."

"Is that why you left New Orleans? Were you Crazy Eve back there?" Corinne patted her hand.

"You are such a brat." Eve couldn't help laughing. "No, I didn't run over the jerk, and please don't tell Callum you suspected it. He'd have a field day with that."

"Have you met Martha yet?" Corinne asked.

Eve paused, thinking.

"In her sixties or so. Short, brown hair?" Corinne supplied more information.

"That rings a bell," Eve nodded. "Is she as mischievous as she looks?"

Corinne nodded, laughing. "And then some. She was my favorite teacher in junior high. I swear she sticks around just to keep this town on its toes. You'll love her."

Ian brought their food, effectively ending the conversation. Eve was too ravenous to divert her attention from the feast in front of her. Wherever the fish had come from, it was scrumptious.

Whether the topic was truly put to rest or it was only on temporary hiatus, the remainder of the meal passed without mention of Callum. Mostly, Corinne pointed out various patrons and filled Eve in on the gossip around them. They made a game out of speculating about the more mysterious ones.

Some part of Eve was tempted to linger after if to do nothing more than sit in a corner booth and watch the everyday stories unfold around her in real-time. But she was also covered in paint and her introverted spirit was on people overload.

So, after paying for her meal, Eve said her goodbyes and went to celebrate her last night in her room at the Kelpie with a hot bath and her favorite book, *Sense and Sensibility*. She had it mostly memorized, but there was something comforting about the familiar words.

The next morning, she hopped out of bed with more zeal than usual. It didn't take long to get ready or to gather her things and check out of the hotel. She arrived at the Dragonfly early, eager to run a few loads of things up to her apartment before her shift began in the store. Eve stopped short when she reached her landing, her fingers loosening their grip on the suitcase handle in her surprise.

She was so busy inspecting the ornate iron bed that had magically appeared on her stoop that she didn't even realize her bag had tumbled back down the stairs until she heard the telltale thud and swearing that meant she'd manage to injure Callum again. The corner of her mouth twitched. She knew she shouldn't laugh, but a small chuckle just couldn't be helped.

He appeared a moment later, holding her suitcase out to her. "I suppose this is yours."

"Yes, thank you so much." She barely looked up, mostly because she didn't trust herself not to laugh again; he was so endearingly irritated.

"I'm fine. Thank you for asking. I mean, it'll probably bruise, but I'm fine."

"What'll bruise?" Eve's eyebrows knit together.

He huffed in response. Eve did grin at that, realizing it was a game of sorts—she considered it a win when she made him do the angry bear huff.

"Do you know where the bed came from?"

He scowled and opened his mouth to respond before closing his mouth and taking a deep breath. When he did speak, his entire demeanor had changed again. "No idea."

"Why do you think it's here?"

"It has your name on it." He pointed.

"How did I not notice that?"

"I don't even want to hazard a guess."

Eve cut her eyes over at him. "Uh-huh. Did you do this?"

"Why would I give you furniture? You abuse me."

She stood back and folded her arms across her chest. "Well, who would do this?"

"Maybe it's a housewarming gift."

"Last time I got someone a housewarming gift it was a candle set."

"Maybe we're friendlier here."

"I don't even know what to say." Eve blinked, her eyes suspiciously watery.

"Why don't I help you get it inside?" he suggested.

"Yeah, thanks. I'm going to be late for work." She glanced at her watch, out of habit more than necessity. She'd been pushing it on time when she'd first come up; she was unquestionably late by this point.

"I have an in with your boss; I can put in a good word for you if needed." The smile he graced her with was so charming all coherent thought skittered out of her brain, if only for the briefest of moments.

"Thanks." She smiled back, her feet momentarily rooted to their spot before she shook it off and unlocked the door. Eve tucked her suitcase in the closet and turned to help get the bed, but he waved her off.

"Nope. I got this."

Eve would have argued, but they both knew it was out of self-preservation. If she got involved with the move, he'd somehow wind up injured. Instead, she merely thanked him and stood back out of the way. She didn't even trust herself to go get a load from the car. For some reason, where Callum was concerned, it was best just to keep her distance. The pair of them was a magnet for pain and she couldn't help wondering if that was metaphorical.

CHAPTER 5

Callum had been right. The instant Moira had seen Eve and Callum walking down the stairs together, her frown had disappeared, and she never said a word about Eve's tardiness on her fourth day of work. Eve tried a few times to offer an explanation—and to dispel any misconceptions Moira might have—but she'd been waved off each time. She was starting to get annoyed with that particular McTavish gesture.

But there was enough work to be done to leave little room for any unnecessary conversation, so Eve eventually gave up and threw herself into preparing the store for the festival happening the next day. She'd been told it was the best of the area's food and wine, and the entire town was bracing for the influx of people that would hit by this evening.

Personally, Eve wondered how Moira would have gotten everything ready if she hadn't been there. As it was, they barely finished the last display by the time Lily came in for her shift. Though Eve thought the tall, willowy teen was much prettier than she'd been, the girl reminded her of herself in high school. She seemed to be liked well enough but was happiest perched on a stool in an antique store, reading a book.

Today, there would be no reading. Being a town native, she

instinctively stashed her schoolbooks and got straight to work. Eve felt bad leaving, but Moira shooed her off.

"You've put in a full day, and I know you still have your car to unpack. Go. We've got this."

Eve thanked her and promised to be back bright and early to help set up their outdoor display before snagging another box from her car and scurrying up the stairs. Her stoop hadn't conjured any new furniture, but she hadn't expected it to. She was thrilled with the bed, and she adored the robin's egg blue sheets and comforter that she ventured out for after dinner. It was all so sinfully soft, she was pretty sure she'd found Nirvana when she stretched her toes out under the blankets for the first time.

She felt only marginally guilty for bowing out of the invitations she'd received for the night, choosing instead to curl up with the fictional characters dancing through her brain. She needed to recuperate after so much peopling.

As much as she relished the quiet, there was a twinge of something new: loneliness. Someone to share the quiet moments with. Callum flashed through her mind, but she batted the image away. Her one attempt at a lasting relationship had left her trapped in a web of lies and narcissistic maneuverings. She wasn't keen to return to that mire.

But she could get a dog. The idea was a foreign one to her. She'd never even owned a goldfish. Meeting Sadie made her consider the notion, though. Eve fell asleep that night curled up with her pillow and daydreaming about adding a canine to her life. After all, wasn't this entire adventure about trying new things?

The next morning, she got to work early in hopes of asking Moira about her pet policy.

"Oh good! You're here." The woman in question was a blur who paused only long enough to transfer a box into Eve's arms. "Can you take these outside to Callum?"

Of course, she mentally groaned. Outwardly, she smiled. "Sure thing."

She backed through the door, doing her best to not damage the contents of the box in her arms. He greeted her with a bright grin and a cheerful hello.

"I come bearing gifts." She lifted the box a skosh higher.

"Cool. Just put it over there." He motioned with his head, his hands already occupied as he struggled to stretch a cloth across the display table.

Eve set the box down and scurried to help, earning another grin and a "Thanks."

"What do we have going on here?" Eve asked.

Callum stopped working to survey his progress. "The Dragonfly has a much better location for the festival, so we set up the booth for the Mortal Kelpie here. Using things from the Dragonfly, of course, so when people comment about liking the serving dish or whatever, we can tell them where to buy their own."

"Makes sense." Eve paused, then decided to ask the question that had been on her mind for a while. "What does the bar's name mean? I know what a kelpie is. But why mortal?"

Callum chuckled. "It's Scottish slang. For drunk."

"And shattered?"

"Exhausted."

"Clever."

"Pop thought so," Callum said. "He was pretty proud of the names."

Eve thought to herself that she'd like to meet the McTavish parents. The pair settled into an easy rhythm, working side-by-side to put the display together. For the first time since she'd nearly run him over, she felt comfortable in his presence. Maybe it was having a familiar task to ground her. Maybe she was finally relaxing around him. Either way, by the time Moira came out to check on them, Eve was putting the finishing touches on the display and she was enjoying herself immensely.0000000000

"Oh my! This is lovely," Moira exclaimed, clapping her hands together.

"Yeah?" Eve stepped back to admire her handiwork as Callum plugged in the white twinkle lights.

"Oh sweetheart, it's darling."

Eve flushed with pride in response.

Callum came to stand behind the women; Eve could almost feel the rumble of his voice as he spoke. "Aunt Moira, you should let Eve go check out the festival before it gets started. This is her first one, you know."

"That's okay—" Eve's protest was interrupted by her boss.

"That's a great idea!" Moira's eyes lit up. "Why don't you show her around, Callum?"

Eve opened her mouth to launch a new protest, but the beseeching look on Callum's face softened her. What possible reason could she have for not wanting to explore the festival with a handsome man? The fact that she hesitated made Eve question her sanity.

"Sure."

"Really?" Callum's eyebrows shot up.

"Yeah. Sounds fun." She even allowed him to snag her hand and lead her away. Eve tried to take it all in, the sights, the sounds, the smells. She tried to make small talk with vendors. But all she could seem to focus on was the warmth of his hand enveloping hers. It's not like the contact created some magic spark, but it was hard to concentrate on anything other than his nearness or the warmth it was creating in the pit of her belly.

Eve paused in front of a store window full of random knick-knacks, pointing to a grizzly bear figurine. "This is cute."

Callum huffed. "Cute."

"You don't like it?"

"Bears and cute are not two words that go together."

"Are you kidding? They're adorable!"

"They are killing machines. Have you seen their claws?"

"You're serious?"

"Absolutely. Those things are terrifying."

His aversion to bears amused Eve greatly, given that she'd always mentally compared him to the very same. "How wrong is it that I kind of want to buy you this bear now?"

"Very wrong." He didn't miss a beat.

"Then I'll resist the temptation… for now."

His chuckle was rich and deep, and it warmed her from the inside out. She racked her brain for something to say, something that would keep this moment alive. His cell phone vibrated before anything came to mind, though. He frowned at the screen. "Looks like reality is beckoning. Ian needs me to grab a case of beer he forgot at the Kelpie. Can you find your way back to the Dragonfly?"

"Yep." Eve nodded, trying to hide her disappointment.

"You positive?"

Eve smiled. His concern made her happy. "Absolutely positive. Go help your family. I have to get to work, too. Thank you for a lovely time."

He started to pull away and then paused, looking down into her eyes. She tried to read his expression. She wasn't sure she dared to interpret it, but the look on his face made her feel special, treasured even. Callum leaned in, brushing a kiss against her forehead. "Have a good day, cutie."

"You too, handsome." She couldn't help it, she watched him go, marveling at the shift between them. She spent the rest of her walk back sifting through their time together, turning each moment over in her mind, relishing how very happy they made her.

Ian was at the booth already when she arrived, setting up the food.

"I heard you did this," he said when he noticed her approach. "It looks amazing."

"Thanks." She flushed with pride. "Do you need help?"

"Yeah, that would be great. Things were too busy for Corrine to get away from the Kelpies and we're already short-staffed, so it's just me."

"Sure thing. Just let me check in with Moira. I'll be right back."

He answered with a nod, barely looking up as he moved through a routine he seemed to know by heart.

Moira was more than happy to have Eve help out with the booth and to be a runner, assuring her that she and Lily could handle the store.

Working with Ian was fun. His easygoing nature helped her forget she was an introvert. She didn't see much more of Callum, except in passing as the two of them bounced between the Dragonfly and the Kelpie, shuttling supplies and pitching in wherever they needed them most.

The evening was an odd mix of running into familiar faces, people she'd met over the past week, while not quite fitting into any of the groups. It left her feeling both isolated and like she could belong here if she tried. For the first time, she wanted to try.

It was only a few hours long, but her legs and back were still aching by the time the event was over. And while she longed for a bubble bath and her bed, she accepted Corinne's invitation to check out the live music and street dancing. This was, after all, why she'd moved halfway across the country: to build a life.

They'd spent the evening feeding everyone else, but none of them had eaten all day, so Corinne brought them dinner from the Kelpie when her shift was over at the inn. The four of them snagged a table and ate in companionable silence. There was nothing awkward about it; they were all simply so tired and hungry that their brains couldn't focus on anything other than how good the food was.

As the sun set, strings of lights came on, bobbing like fireflies in the breeze. The band started up, and Eve couldn't help thinking it was an entirely pleasant evening. Now that she had food in her belly, she could be quite content to sit and people watch all evening.

Corinne had no such inclination. "Which one of my brothers is going to dance with me?"

"Always." Ian got to his feet with a charming grin, holding a hand out to his sister.

"You say that now, but someday some woman is going to steal your heart, and then I'll be left without a dance partner."

"You could date, you know," Ian reminded her.

"I'm so busy that God would have to literally drop a man in my lap for that to happen." The pair continued their conversation as they disappeared into the crowd.

"Would you like to dance?" Callum asked.

Eve smiled and shook her head. "It's very gallant of you to ask, but you don't have to. I'm enjoying this."

"Eve." Callum stood, offering a hand out to her. "I'm asking because I want to dance with a beautiful woman. Not because I have to."

Startled, she looked at his hand, considering for the briefest of moments before putting her hand in his. "Okay."

"Just don't step on my toes. I don't think they're healed from the bookcase yet."

"You are such a baby."

"You're a one-woman demolition crew."

"Smooth talker," she accused, even as he pulled her neatly into his arms.

Even after a long day, he still smelled good. Surely he'd gone home to clean up first. That made Eve wonder how she smelled since she hadn't thought to run home and shower in between. And, for a moment, panic flared. But the heat from his embrace soon made all thoughts skitter right out of her brain, replaced by a slow burn she hadn't felt in a very long time.

They didn't talk, she simply rested her head on his chest and soaked it all in as the couple moved to the music. It was… bliss.

And then the song changed, the slow, sultry beat giving way

to something bouncy. The couple took a step back, Callum's expression matching the swirl of emotions she felt inside. Before either could speak, Molly appeared, tugging at Eve's hand.

"Come on. Dance with us."

Without waiting for a response, the woman tugged Eve toward a gaggle of women of various ages, all dancing as if nobody was watching in the middle of the street. Eve looked back at Callum helplessly, but he just shrugged. He was obviously not going to be any help.

At first, she swayed awkwardly and not necessarily on the beat, looking to the other women for some sort of guidance. She couldn't remember the last time she'd danced. Corinne joined the group, giving Eve a quick side-hug and a word of encouragement. "Close your eyes. Forget anyone else. Just move how your body wants to move."

"I have never done that in my life," Eve admitted.

"I know. Give it a try." With one last squeeze, Corinne moved to the center of the group, joining hands with Martha as the two women did a silly dance together with utter abandon.

Eve envied their ease, so she tried to do as Corinne suggested, closing her eyes and focusing on the music. Before long, her hips began to move, and then her arms. Some part of her worried that she was inventing a new dance that would come to be known as the flailing fish, but then she reassured herself that it might be nice to give the townspeople something to talk about besides the infamous coin toss, so she went with it.

By the second song, she and Molly were bouncing around with their own stupid little dance, and she was laughing so hard her sides hurt. Two more songs and they slowed it down again. Callum was there, materializing out of thin air to claim her hand.

"I'll dance, but only if you prop me up," she told him. "I'm pretty sure my legs are melting."

"I was beginning to wonder if I was ever going to get you back from those ladies."

"That was unexpectedly fun," she admitted.

"I could tell."

"If I looked ridiculous, don't tell me. I don't want to know."

"You most definitely did not look ridiculous," he assured her, sending a new wave of warmth rushing through her.

As sad as Eve was when the evening was done, she was also incredibly relieved to crawl into bed. She'd hoped to take the next day to recuperate, but it was another busy day at work and Corinne insisted she meet the McTavish siblings at the Kelpie for burgers and fries for dinner to celebrate a successful festival. After the past couple of days, she probably needed red meat more than she needed sleep anyway.

Ian brought out four mugs of ale as the four of them settled into a booth. The frothy drink was a new one for Eve, but she found it delightful—from the way the foam tickled her lip to the slightly chocolatey, nutty taste. The lower the ale got in the mugs, the more she forgot how tired she was. Conversation got rowdier and Eve was happy to find she wasn't watching the conversation, she was in the thick of it.

"You've got to stop treating our guests like they're your very own soap opera," Callum teased his sister.

"Then they should stop being so interesting," she countered.

"Are they, though?" Ian asked.

"Come on. Take those two, for instance." She nodded in the direction of a couple sitting in a back corner, completely immersed in each other. "They are most definitely not married to each other, but they're both wearing rings."

"How can you tell they're not married? Because they're getting along?"

Eve couldn't help wondering if the cynicism in Callum's voice just then should be a red flag. Instead, she found herself answering his question. "Their rings don't match, for one. His is black tungsten and silver. Hers is rose gold. And the styles are totally different."

"I'm not sure that's enough to base your theory on." Callum wasn't sold.

"No, she's right," Corinne argued. "Nobody buys clashing wedding rings. If they're married to each other, I'm dying to know the story."

"You two are going to be dangerous together, aren't you?" Ian chuckled.

"Seriously, look at their body language," Corinne persisted. "Look at the tension between them. They haven't done the deed yet."

"Done the deed." Callum rolled his eyes. "Are we back in junior high?"

Corinne stuck her tongue out at him

"It warms my heart to see some things never change." A new voice cut into the conversation.

Eve looked up and nearly choked on her drink. Wes Dryden was smiling charmingly down at their table, his black eyes practically dancing with amusement. Eve had never been that close to a celebrity before. She tried to play it cool, but her brain was an explosion of colliding thoughts. Did her hair look okay? Did she have something in her teeth? Was her breath funky from dinner? Could he even smell it? And most importantly: Why was this actor popping by their table?

He was even better looking in person than on the small screen, with a nearly-tangible charisma that added to his appeal. Eve forced herself to look away and realized Callum was half watching her even as he answered Wes. She couldn't quite tell what the expression was on his face, amusement or irritation.

"Good to see you, Wes. I didn't know you were back in the States."

"Finally. The shutdowns put us crazy behind schedule, but we just wrapped. They let us sneak home for a quick break."

"And you chose to spend it with us?" Callum didn't attempt to hide his amused disbelief.

"I happen to like this little lake town of yours, my friend. But no, I chose to spend it with my girl. I ran down to pick up dinner while she got settled in."

"Your girl?" Corinne butted into the conversation. "I didn't know you had a girl. Who is it? Anyone I know?"

Wes gave a sly grin. "Nobody you know, but you will. We'll let the press catch wind sooner or later, and when we do, I will most definitely bring her by to meet you. But for now, we're here to hide. We haven't seen each other in ages; we have a bit of catching up to do."

"Got it. We'll keep it quiet," Callum promised.

"Thanks," Wes said before turning his attention to the other McTavish. "It's good to see you, man."

"You, too. Maybe next visit we can grab a beer."

"I'd like that. Or if you're ever in L.A."

Ian shook his head. "That was Callum's scene."

"Hi, I'm Wes." It took Eve a moment to realize he was talking to her.

"Eve. I'm Eve." She mentally kicked herself for tripping over her name.

He took her hand, looking from Eve to Callum and back again. "It's nice to meet you, Eve."

"Eve just moved here," Corinne explained.

"Did you? How do you like it so far?"

"It's lovely. Very different from home." Eve tried to think of something else to say but couldn't for the life of her think of how to sum up her time here so far.

"And where's home?"

"Well, here, now, I guess. But it was New Orleans."

"Laissez les bons temps rouler." His grin was pure devilish delight.

Eve couldn't help smiling back. "Oui, cher."

"Now I see why Callum wouldn't introduce you; he's trying to keep you all to himself." He winked at her. Eve's heart hit her throat. *The* Wes Dryden winked at her.

"I just didn't get a chance," Callum defended himself.

"Right." Wes smirked, clearly amused at the chaos he'd wrought. "I'd better get upstairs before her dinner gets cold. She gets mean when she's hungry."

They all said their goodbyes, Eve still reeling over meeting him in the first place. As soon as Wes was out of earshot, Callum turned to her.

"What the hell was that?"

"That was Wes Dryden. I thought you knew him." Eve was genuinely perplexed.

"Not that… you. Were you flirting with him?" The amount of indignation in his voice amused her.

"I don't know. Was I?" This time Eve deliberately goaded him.

"A little." Corinne giggled. "But it's hard not to with him."

"I was just being nice." Eve shrugged. "He's easy to talk to."

"Huh." Was the only response she got from Callum, though she was left with the distinct impression he had more he wanted to say.

"Who do you think the girl is?" Corinne was practically vibrating with curiosity.

Eve tried to remember the latest gossip on him. "Wasn't he dating a girl from Kansas or Oklahoma or something?"

"Surely not. That was forever ago. Definitely pre-pandemic." Corinne shook her head. "I think I heard they got stuck in different countries when things shut down."

"Maybe they made long-distance work," Eve speculated.

Corinne was skeptical. "Does anybody ever actually make that work?"

"He did say he hadn't seen her in ages," Ian interjected.

Callum frowned. "Don't encourage them."

"He's from Hollywood. Ages probably means a week." Corinne's voice carried an air of authority Eve wasn't sure it deserved. "I think he's seeing that one actress… the pretty one… you know…"

"Aren't they all pretty?" Callum asked, earning a look from both women that clearly said, "You poor, simple man."

"The one with the phenomenal bone structure," Corinne continued trying to place the actress she was thinking of.

"Oh! That was the villain in that thing? Yes!" Eve could picture her but couldn't put a name to the face. "Yeah, I do think I saw something on Insta about them."

"It's like you two have a language all your own," Ian marveled.

"You say that like it's a good thing," Callum mused.

"It is impressive."

"What I'm wondering is how you know Wes Dryden." Eve circled the conversation back to the question foremost on her mind. "Was he a guest here before or something?"

"Nah, he was Callum's roommate in college," Ian supplied.

"But we do get famous people here from time to time," Corinne added. "I still swear that was Rob Pattinson."

Callum sighed heavily at his sister, as if they'd had the conversation before. "That was not Rob Pattinson."

"I'm the one who talked to him. I'm telling you it was him."

The pair devolved into bickering and eventually, the conversation moved on until Eve brought it grinding to a halt again when the topic of water skiing came up and she admitted she'd never been.

"Wait, wait, wait—you've never been water skiing?" Ian's look was incredulous.

Corinne reached out and smacked him upside the head. "Way to make her feel bad about it." She turned to Eve. "It's okay. I'm sure there are lots of people who've never been water skiing."

Eve wasn't sure the patronizing tone helped much, but the larger-than-life personalities that ran in this family were part of their charm. It stood to reason that the flip side of those personalities were moments like this. So, she sucked up her pride, shook her head, and answered frankly. "Nope, I'm a water-skiing virgin."

"Then please, let me be there for your first." The look in Callum's eyes made her regret her choice of words.

Eve's face flushed; she rolled her eyes to hide her embarrassment. "If you must." And somehow, without her being exactly sure how it had happened, plans were made to take her skiing for the first time.

When dinner was finished, Eve found she was a little wobbly on her feet. Perhaps, at 5'3", she shouldn't have tried to keep up with the 6' tall men drinking ale.

His expression amused, Callum offered her his arm. "Mind if I walk you home?"

"I think that's a good idea." Eve licked her lips. He was such an attractive man. Maybe it was a terrible idea to let him walk her home. What if she embarrassed herself and jumped him the instant they got to her door?

They didn't talk much on the way back. His long fingers were laced through hers as they wandered back toward the Dragonfly. The breeze kissed her skin; lights bobbed happily on the water in the distance. She couldn't be sure if it was the alcohol or the man that made her feel so warm and fuzzy from head to toe. Either way, Eve was happy. This was a good moment. The kind you tuck away to remember later.

They arrived at her door sooner than she would have liked. Eve fumbled with her lock for a moment before he turned her back toward him. With the door at her back and him so close in front of her, she was even less certain of her ability to control what happened next. She wanted him, so much it scared her. There was something almost animalistic in the need; it was palpable in the air between them. Her breath became jagged. She was suspended in a moment of choice, lured by the delicious pull of him yet afraid to yield.

His face moved toward her, and her decision was made. "Goodnight," she blurted as she pushed through to the safety of her loft, closing the door firmly in his face. *Oh, dear Lord, what had she done?* However big of a fool she'd just made of herself,

Eve knew she wouldn't have stopped at just a kiss. She'd have pulled Callum McTavish into her apartment and... she let her imagination take over from there.

The rest of her night was a restless one. Eve would drift off to sleep only to be awoken by unsettling dreams. She was always running from something in them. She was in danger—it was a different danger every time, but the peril was constant.

By the time she slunk down the stairs to work the next morning, she was grateful for the caffeine and the sunshine to help put the whole crazy night behind her. If Callum's greeting was a bit cooler than usual, Eve couldn't blame him. She had, after all, closed the door in his face.

After the first day, he thawed a bit and stopped avoiding her quite so obviously. She couldn't be sure if it was because of the bear figurine left in a gift bag in his front seat, hoping to make him smile. She couldn't even be sure if he'd gotten it; he'd never said either way. Still, it was apparent things had shifted between them again. He was certainly more guarded than he had been before.

The week passed quickly enough either way, and Eve had no shortage of people popping by the store to say hi. One or two might have even been there to flirt, though she'd never been super great at picking up on that. An older woman named Gale most certainly came by to size her up. Three minutes into the conversation and Eve had her pegged as the town gossip.

She also had more furniture mysteriously appear on her stoop. First a dresser, and then a TV stand—which amused her because she didn't own a television. Next was an overstuffed chair perfect for curling up and reading in. Eve asked Moira if she knew where the furniture came from.

"If you need furniture, just go see Larry down at the furniture store. Tell him I sent you and he'll take care of you."

It did nothing to help her solve the mystery, but Eve made a mental note to go ask the man if he knew who her benefactor was. But then furniture stopped appearing and life got busy, and Eve never quite got around to following up on her lead.

Their skiing date rolled around before Eve was ready. The more she thought about it, the more nervous she was about agreeing to strap wood to her feet and allow herself to be dragged behind a boat at high speeds. It just didn't seem logical.

"You'll do great," Corinne reassured her for the tenth time as she helped Eve secure her life vest. Her friend's encouragement bolstered Eve long enough to get her out of the boat. But as she bobbed in the water, waiting for them to circle around with the rope, she began to question her life choices. Once she had rope in hand, there was nothing left to do but signal that she was good to go and hold on for dear life.

The boat moved forward, the rope went taut, and Eve found herself lifted out of the water as if by magic. The tension began to ebb away, and she even came close to enjoying the experience. That is, until she found herself tumbling through the air before plunging into the unforgiving wall of water. She came up sputtering, wondering where on earth her skis had gone.

The boat circled around, coming to a stop a short distance from her. Eve couldn't help wincing as she sliced through the water toward the ladder. Everything hurt—a fact made even more evident when she lifted herself onto the boat.

Callum must have seen the look on her face because he was there in an instant, examining her for injuries and asking where it hurt.

"I'm fine. Nothing is more wounded than my pride." She tried to assure him as she fought with her life vest.

He reached up to take over the task. "Here. Let me."

And she did, not having the energy to fight it.

"That was not as fun as I was led to believe it would be."

"Are you kidding?" Ian glanced over his shoulder at her. "That wipeout was phenomenal!"

"I aim to please." Eve ran her hands down her legs. She wasn't sure why she did it, maybe to reassure herself they were still intact. The boat lurched as Ian kicked it into gear, steering toward the shoreline. Callum reached out to steady her, even as Eve grabbed his arms to do the same.

"You want to go again?" Corinne asked.

"Nope, I'm good."

Ian stopped the boat again to retrieve a ski. "Are you sure? It takes a few tries to get a feel for it."

"I think I've experienced enough new things for one week." Eve held her ground.

"Come ride in the front with me." Corinne offered. "That's more fun than skiing anyway."

Eve wanted to ask why they hadn't started with that, but let it go. The women made themselves comfortable on the bench seats on either side of the front, lying back against the boat's windshield and basking in the sun as the wind and water spray cooled them. Every so often, Ian would cross another boat's wake, causing a wall of water to douse them. They'd squeal and he'd laugh. Eve enjoyed it all immensely.

They stopped at a little island for a picnic lunch. It was funny how much better cold cuts tasted after an afternoon of sunshine and water and wind. As the afternoon ebbed, conversation flowed and the last of the tension between Eve and Callum dissipated, leaving a happy glow in its stead.

CHAPTER 6

*E*ve existed in a happy little bubble for the next few days, finding they had a pleasant rhythm to them now that she was settling into her new home. There was no shortage of interesting places to grab a light breakfast and a cup of coffee, so Eve made her rounds through each of them. It was an enjoyable place to people watch, and she found herself saying hello to more people each day.

She learned to stay away from the bakery on Saturdays because that's when Gale's women's group met. Eve told herself she was judging the woman too harshly; she was probably a perfectly decent human. Still, she gave off a pious vibe that Eve was inclined to steer clear of, so she ate at home on Saturdays or went to the coffee truck. The café was too packed to be an option on weekends.

After breakfast, she'd go for a walk around the square before clocking in at work. Lunch, she spent reading—if she remembered to take lunch at all. Callum's daily visit to the store had become something to look forward to, now that his surly demeanor had been replaced by a softer countenance. He might not smile as easily as Ian, but something about that made it all the more rewarding when he did. Eve couldn't help wondering if the difference between them was as simple as personality or if something had happened to make Callum the more reserved of the two brothers.

More often than not, she found her way down to the Kelpie to eat dinner with the McTavish siblings. She'd always tell herself she was going to eat in, but then Corinne would text about 2 p.m. to invite her over. If she resisted then, it only meant Callum would pop by an hour or two later to plead his sister's case. And while she did enjoy seeing him, Eve found it easiest to just accept the initial invitation most nights.

Dinner with the McTavish siblings was rowdier than she was used to, having grown up an only child. So often, it was only her and her mother at dinner, and her mother was never especially known for her conversation. Sometimes, Eve had the passing thought that it might have been nice to grow up with a mother like Moira, but it was a fleeting thought that left her feeling guilty. Her mom had been a kind and gentle soul. She'd kept to herself, but still somehow managed to spread kindness wherever she went, if in her own, understated way.

In their short time together, Eve had learned that Moira was divorced and not even a little inclined to remarry. Her evenings were often filled with book clubs, political activism, cultural events, and the occasional date. But every so often, on a night like this one, she'd link arms with Eve and the pair would take a meandering walk toward the bar, discussing anything and nothing as they went. Eve particularly enjoyed those evenings.

"You're in for a treat tonight," Moira promised as they set out.

Eve's curiosity was instantly piqued. "Why's that?"

"My brother and sister-in-law are home."

"Corinne didn't mention that." Eve's steps faltered. Her anxiety skyrocketed at the thought of meeting Callum's parents. She admonished herself for being silly. They weren't a couple; there was no special weight to meeting his mom. Still, she spent the rest of the short walk mentally debating what to call her. The

McTavish matriarch was affectionately known as Mama McT to most of the town, but the nickname felt too familiar. Sorcha, her given name, might be more appropriate. As it turned out, she could have saved herself the mental energy.

Eve wasn't used to people disliking her. Being indifferent or overlooking her entirely, perhaps, but she couldn't recall anyone ever having a blatant distaste for her. She felt it rather unfortunate that her first encounter with the experience was with Callum's mother.

After a cold appraisal that apparently found Eve wanting, the woman informed her she could call her Mrs. McTavish. That declaration was the closest Mama McT came to being rude. She was, for the most part, polite to Eve, sometimes even bordering on pleasant. But even the pleasant conversations left Eve blinking, wondering if she'd just been insulted.

After the disaster that meeting Mama McT had been, she braced for the worst when Callum's father made his appearance. The burly man had a warm, almost jovial energy about him, scooping his sister up in a big ol' bear hug despite her protests.

When he turned his attention to Eve, she reflexively held a hand out to shake, hoping to ward off a hug. She must have telegraphed her motives because he chuckled as he accepted the greeting, his massive paw completely enveloping her tiny hand.

"You must be Eve. I'm delighted to meet you. Sorry I wasn't here sooner; I was getting the car unpacked so I don't have to deal with it later."

Relief washed over her at the warm reception. "I'm so happy to meet you, too, sir."

"Please, call me Angus." He released her hand but not her gaze. "You have caused quite the stir with your arrival, my dear. Although I have to say, you're even prettier than Callum said."

Eve was saved having to think of a reply to that by Callum's shout from across the bar. "Really, Dad?"

"What?" He shrugged innocently. "It's my job to embarrass you, isn't it? Later, I'll break out the bad jokes."

"I can hardly wait." Corinne stood on tiptoe to kiss his cheek as she passed by.

"They're pretty punny," he quipped, to which Corinne rolled her eyes and Eve giggled.

"Come on, Eve, I need your help grabbing plates."

"I don't know that you should be letting a stranger in the kitchen," Sorcha frowned.

Corinne rolled her eyes a second time, reminding Eve of a teenager. "Eve isn't a stranger, Mom."

"I don't think your mom likes me very much," Eve confided once they were alone.

"Don't mind her. She's just being a mama bear over Callum. It's weird, I know. He's thirty-five."

Eve wasn't quite sure what to make of that, so she let the subject drop, holding out her hands to accept the stack of plates Corinne was handing her. Even though these dinners were held at the pub, they took over a back corner table and treated it like a family meal. Eve realized with a start she'd never seen any of the McTavish's homes. She wondered in passing if they even had homes or if they lived at the Kelpies.

"So, dear brother," Moira leaned over to get Angus's attention. "Tell me all about Greece."

"It was sunny." He shrugged, grabbing a dinner roll from the basket Corinne was setting on the table.

"You have such a lovely way with words." Moira turned her attention to Sorcha. "So, dear sister-in-law, tell me about Greece."

"We stayed in the most charming little villa in Corfu. The ocean was right out our window. The patio was to die for—there was this little yellow hammock on the patio that was a perfect reading spot."

"That sounds like something you'd like, Eve," Callum interjected. "Eve loves to read."

"It does sound heavenly," Eve agreed.

"How nice." Mama McT barely glanced her way before continuing her story.

Eve gave Callum a smile; it was nice of him to try. The rest of the dinner passed well enough, although the shine was certainly gone from the evening. For the first time since she'd started coming to these dinners, Eve felt like she was on the outside looking in. And for the first time, she was happy when she could politely excuse herself to head home.

"Hey, Eve, wait up," Callum called out when she would have slipped out the door after saying her goodbyes.

"What's up?" She paused, turning back toward him.

"There's no way I'm letting you walk home alone," he told her.

"I walk home alone lots. It's not far."

"Yeah, well, not tonight." He turned his attention to his family. "I'll catch you guys tomorrow. Love you, Mom and Pop."

"But we haven't seen you in over a month," Sorcha protested.

"And it will be so nice to catch up tomorrow. You should swing by the cabin for coffee. I'll make us pancakes." His offer seemed to placate her. It also answered a question for Eve: He did, in fact, have a home.

"You didn't have to walk me home," Eve told him again as they meandered in the general direction of her apartment.

"I know. But I wanted to."

They walked in companionable silence. Eve, for her part, was happy to soak in the evening air and the warmth of his presence. Her hand itched to take his, but thoughts of how mortified she'd be if he asked her what she was doing kept her from acting on the impulse.

When they came to a stop in front of the Dragonfly, he was the one to take her hand as he turned to face her. "I'd like to make you dinner tomorrow."

"What?" She'd heard him, she was just struggling to process the words.

"Dinner. Tomorrow. I can cook—and I will be a perfect gentleman, scout's honor."

"You were a scout?"

"No. Never. But I promise, just dinner. I'm not inviting you over for a hookup or anything. We're just always surrounded by a group. It's hard to get to know each other."

He wasn't wrong about that. "Okay. Dinner sounds good."

"Any food allergies or anything I should know about?"

"Nope. But I do have an unnatural hatred of brussels sprouts."

"No brussels sprouts. Got it." He grinned and she found herself grinning like a fool back at him. "I'll text you the address, okay?"

"Sounds good."

Eve wore a dopey smile the rest of the evening—at least so long as she didn't dwell on Mama McT's reaction to her. Occasionally, anxiety would rear its ugly head and she'd start to overthink every single interaction with the woman, but then she'd take a deep breath and force herself to focus on the fact that Callum had asked her on a real date.

It had been a long time since Eve had been on a date. Online dating had been an abysmal experience thanks to her inability to make small talk. And antique stores weren't exactly brimming with eligible bachelors in their thirties. It didn't help that she was a natural homebody and had never had much interest in the party scene. So, yeah, it had been a while since she'd been on a proper date.

Her euphoria lasted the rest of the evening and throughout the next day. She struggled to concentrate on actual work all day, grateful for a job that didn't necessarily care if she stayed busy as long as the store was clean and customers were happy. The clock was painfully slow, but time did eventually pass, and Eve found herself standing in front of her closet, bemoaning the complete lack of anything worthwhile to wear.

She remembered the dress she'd seen in the window of the

boutique on Main Street. It was an adorable emerald green wrap dress with the perfect amount of ruffle to it—feminine but not ridiculously so. Knowing they'd be closing any minute, she grabbed her wallet and raced down to the store, reaching the front door just as the sign was being flipped to closed.

Eve's shoulders fell and she mentally berated herself for not buying the dress when she'd first seen it two days ago. At some point, she needed more in her closet than peasant skirts and tank tops.

"Hey," the woman from the store called out, catching Eve's attention just as she'd turned away in defeat. "Did you have something in particular you were looking for?"

"I was hoping to get the green dress," Eve responded. "I have a date tonight."

The adorable blonde smiled and opened the door a little wider. "Well, I would not want to be the one to stand in the way of the perfect date outfit. Come on in."

"Oh my goodness, thank you, thank you, thank you. I will be quick." She made a beeline for the dress rack.

"You're Eve, right? You work over at the Dragonfly?"

"That's me." Eve was unnerved that the woman knew her name.

"I'm Jenna. Jenna Morgan."

"It's nice to meet you, Jenna." Eve smiled at her before holding the dress up triumphantly. "Found my size."

"Great. Do you need any accessories?"

"No, I've held you up long enough. Thank you, though. And thanks again for doing this. I panicked at how pathetic my closet is."

"This will look amazing on you," Jenna assured her.

"Thanks. I will come back when you're actually open to see about remedying the rest of my wardrobe."

"I'll be here," Jenna promised. "Have fun on your date tonight."

"Thanks!" Eve accepted the bag from Jenna and scurried

back to her apartment. The woman seemed nice. Eve had the passing thought that it would be crazy to have two girlfriends her own age. But then her attention was pulled back to the task at hand: getting ready for her date with Callum.

She hung the dress up on her closet door while she grabbed a quick shower to freshen up. Eve piled her dark hair on top of her head to keep it from getting too ridiculously wet and to keep it out of her way as she carefully applied her makeup, something she rarely did. She even accented her large brown eyes with wings, marveling at women who did this daily—and managed to get both eyes to be completely even. She didn't look like a Picasso or anything, but if Callum looked too closely, he'd probably notice the difference. Thankfully, most men didn't notice those things.

Still, once the dress was on, lipstick was applied, and she let her hair tumble down her back, even Eve had to admit she looked pretty danged nice. The dress had been a good call.

She found his house with relative ease but was not expecting to be so thoroughly enamored with it. The big surly Scot lived in an adorable slate blue house with white trim. It sat right smack on the edge of the lake—so close that she debated for a moment if it was a houseboat or not. Taking off from the driveaway was a long boardwalk that led out to a patio sitting on the lake. She'd call it a dock, but the patio chairs and firepit looked much more inviting than the docks she remembered from her childhood visits to the lake.

Callum appeared in the door, pulling Eve's attention away from the lake. She was relieved to see he'd dressed up, too. It would have been awkward if he'd been in sweats or something. The blue jeans and charcoal gray button-down shirt he wore made her heart do a little flutter. He was clean-shaven and freshly showered, making this the first time she'd seen him without scruff.

"You look beautiful," he told her before inviting her in.

"Thanks." Eve blushed. "So do you."

Callum grinned. "Thanks."

Eve made the conscious decision to not amend her statement to handsome. He actually was beautiful, with his copper-brown hair, bright blue eyes, and perfectly chiseled jawline. She liked that he placed a hand lightly on the small of her back as he guided her through the door and gave her a quick tour.

His home was surprisingly modern, with just enough furniture to be cozy without cluttering the small space. White shiplap covered the walls, nicely complementing the driftwood floors. There was the occasional tchotchke or picture to give her glimpses of his personality, but not many. She smiled to herself when her eyes landed on the grizzly bear figurine she'd bought him sitting on top of his bookshelf. It also wasn't lost on her that he had a fairly impressive array of books filling those shelves, from classics to the latest mystery and even a smattering of nonfiction titles and autobiographies.

"Your home is gorgeous, but I didn't have you pegged as a shiplap kind of guy. I am impressed."

"Guys can't watch HGTV? That feels a little sexist," he teased.

"Duly noted."

"Can I get you a drink?" He moved toward the bar. "Is a martini okay?"

"You McTavish boys and your vermouth." She chuckled softly. "That sounds great. With a twist, please."

"Ah, ordering like a pro."

"Ian has been schooling me."

"Has he now?" If Callum had anything else to add, he left it unsaid.

When he handed her two drinks, she raised an eyebrow. "Will I need both of these to muddle through the evening?"

"One's for me, smartass."

"We'll see." Eve was surprised at her sass. Something about Callum made her relax, made flirting easy.

"Uh-huh." He chuckled. "If you want to take your drinks out

to the patio, I'll be right behind with dinner. Maybe we can negotiate a trade."

"You've got me there."

And he did, too. Dinner was filet mignon and asparagus with twice-baked potatoes. Her mouth literally watered when he set the plate in front of her.

They had no sooner settled when a large, white pelican landed on the railing and looked at Callum expectantly.

"Oh my." Eve couldn't help jumping a little.

"Alba, there's nothing for you. Shoo."

"Alba?" Eve questioned. "Is he yours?"

"In a manner of speaking. I found him tangled up in some fishing line a few years ago and rehabbed him. He's fine now—migrates with his pod and everything. But when he's in town, he stops by. Greedy little beggar."

"And you named him Alba." Eve thought the entire thing was utterly adorable.

"He's not going to leave us alone until I find him something." He scooted back from the table. "I'll be right back."

"You're leaving me alone with him?" she called after Callum when the bird hopped down on the deck and waddled her direction. She'd never realized how large pelicans were until just now.

"You'll be fine. He won't hurt you."

Eve was not sold on the notion. "It's just so… big."

"That's what she said." Callum snickered like an errant schoolboy as he tossed a treat to the waiting bird, earning an eye roll from Eve.

"So, you have a pet pelican named Alba, an impressive reading collection, and you can cook—or is this takeout?" She glanced to him awaiting an answer.

"I cooked." He looked offended.

"Nice. So, tell me something else I don't know about you."

"I can't do that—I'll lose my air of mystery."

"Ah, is that what that is?"

"What I want to know is how someone can just flip a coin and pack up everything they have and move halfway across the country," he veered the conversation back her direction.

"Have you never left Lakeport?"

"Sure, for college. I went to Santa Clara. And then I spent a few years working in the film industry down in LA. But it wasn't for me. I like here. And you dodged the question."

"I guess I'd just painted myself into a corner." She shrugged. "My dad skated long ago. My mom passed away. I'd been so involved in the shop I hadn't taken time to build a life outside of it. So, when the shop was gone, I just decided it was time for a change. Starting fresh somewhere new seemed easier than climbing out of the hole there."

He considered her words for a moment. "That makes a surprising amount of sense."

"It did to me." Eve took another bite of the cheesy goodness that was the twice-baked potato. "Dinner is amazing. You're going to put me in a food coma."

"Corinne told me I had to make a big dinner because you eat a lot."

"I do not eat that much." Eve was offended. "Have you seen her with those donuts?"

He laughed outright. "You two sure were quick to turn on each other."

"As all true friends should be?" Eve couldn't help joining his mirth.

The evening passed much too quickly. They laughed and talked and flirted and time just kind of happened in a blink. When Eve could feel herself getting sleepy, she grudgingly announced it time to go home. Callum walked her to the door and paused.

He brushed her cheek with his knuckles, catching her jaw with this thumb to tip her face up. His eyes searched hers so deeply she felt laid bare before him. She wanted to look away, to hide. But her eyes were locked into place. She wanted to memorize every feature, every nuance of his face, to store each and every detail in her heart. He leaned in, brushing her lips with his, testing, pausing for a breath as if to ask permission.

Eve sighed, leaning into the caress. It was all the encouragement he needed. One arm tightened around her waist. The hand that had rested on her face moved to cup the back of her head. His hands were so large; he was so solid and sure. She felt completely encompassed by him, by this moment, as the kiss deepened. It moved from tender to passionate and back again, weaving a hypnotic spell.

A growl rumbled low in the back of his throat. She absolutely just melted into him. She wanted to devour him, to get closer, to feel more. Her brain was no longer in command of the rest of her —or was at very least rendered incapable of decisions. Powerless to move things along or to stop, she surrendered herself wholly to this one solitary kiss. A kiss that moved her more deeply than the sum of any relationship that had come before.

And then it was over. His forehead rested on hers. They shared the same jagged breath. He smiled at her so brilliantly it coaxed a shy one from her in response.

"Oh, Eve girl, we need to do that more often."

She nodded. She didn't trust herself to speak. She'd gush; she'd say something she wasn't ready to say. All she really knew was she felt incredibly cold outside his embrace. Bereft. The feeling only deepened when she'd gone home, leaving her to curl up in her bed alone, hugging her pillow and mulling over the shared moment. Eve didn't know what lay ahead for the two of them, but she knew things had changed for her. Now that her eyes had been opened to what it felt like to be in the arms of the right man, she'd never settle again. Callum had just raised the bar for men everywhere.

CHAPTER 7

*E*ve awoke to a text from Corinne, asking if she wanted to grab a bite at the diner. She accepted, if for no other reason than to admonish her friend about telling Callum she ate a lot. Of course, that also meant Corinne would want to pump her for information about the date; information she wasn't sure she was ready to give.

Still, she couldn't avoid her only friend forever; that would negate the purpose of moving to California to start a new life— one with people in it. So, Eve got dressed in a pair of harem pants and a loose V-neck t-shirt, pulling her hair into a messy bun and calling it good.

Her heart fell a little when she noticed Corinne's mother was sitting in the chair next to her. She was positive her friend had intentionally neglected to mention that it wouldn't be just the two of them. *Brat*, Eve mentally accused.

To Eve's utter surprise, Mama McT smiled warmly as they all said their hellos. Even better, Corinne didn't bring up the date, and conversation settled into easier territories, like gossip from the staff at the inn and how things were going at Dragonfly.

"Has Moira started getting ready for Splash In yet?" Mama McT surprised Eve by speaking directly to her.

"No." Eve shook her head. "What's Splash In?"

"Seaplanes fly in from all over in September. We have competitions, a barbeque, a wine tasting... it's fun," Mama McT told her.

"That sounds incredibly cool." Eve found herself eagerly looking forward to the event and made a mental note to ask Moira what needed to be done to get the Dragonfly ready.

"Okay, I've been good for as long as I can—" Corinne started, causing Eve's stomach to lurch. She knew where this was headed. "Please tell me all about your date last night. I'm dying to hear every last detail."

"You had a date last night?" Mama McT seemed oddly interested, and maybe even pleased.

"I did." Eve blushed and looked down. "It was lovely. He made us dinner—was a shockingly good cook—and we ate on the patio overlooking the water."

"How nice, dear."

"Did he make the steak? I told him to make the steak." Corinne leaned in, eager for more details.

"He did make the steak—and thanks for telling him I eat a lot, by the way. Everything was pretty perfect. The weather, the music, the stars. And the pelican is adorable. How did I not know he had a pelican?"

"Oh. Callum was your date." The McTavish matriarch's demeanor changed in an instant. "I didn't realize. And you ate at his place?"

"He wanted to have dinner somewhere without a crowd," Eve explained.

"I think it's romantic." Corinne sighed. "He's been tripping over himself since you pulled into town. Please put that man—and all of us—out of misery."

"You're exaggerating," Eve protested, embarrassed.

Corinne waggled her eyebrows mischievously. "Did you stay the night?"

Mama McT's face said she was not amused. She looked

rather horrified at the thought, actually.

"No, I did not stay the night." Eve was also horrified but at the entire situation. "He was a perfect gentleman."

"Too bad." Corinne's shoulders fell. When she saw the look on her mother's face she protested. "What? Mama, he's a grown man."

"I don't care. I still don't want to hear these things."

"No, I'm sorry, if we have to watch you and Pop make googly eyes at each other all the time, you get to hear these conversations."

Eve wouldn't mind being left out of these conversations, not that either McTavish woman would let her get a word in edgewise. She sat and watched them bicker. It was rather like watching a heated tennis match. Eventually, they wore each other out and conversation moved on. Still, it left a knot in the pit of Eve's stomach. As much as she liked Callum—and she genuinely liked the man—she wasn't sure she wanted to be in the middle of a family feud. She certainly didn't want to be the cause of it.

Maybe that's why she didn't reply right away when Callum texted her later to say good morning. She intended to reply soon, but every time she picked her phone up, she'd talk herself out of whatever text she had planned. Before she knew it, it was 6 p.m. and she was closing up the shop.

Having declined Corinne's invite to dinner, she set out for a walk to clear her head. Thirty minutes later, her head was no clearer but her stomach was rumbling, so she picked up some sushi and a bottle of wine from the corner store and headed home with her treasure.

She stopped short at the sight of Callum leaning casually against her door.

"You never texted back," he said by way of greeting.

"I'm sorry." She offered no explanation.

"And you turned down Corinne's invitation to dinner, even though she laid it on pretty thick."

"I just needed some me time."

He nodded slowly, considering her words. "Did I do something?"

"Not at all." She was quick to reassure him. "You've been quite charming."

"Was it dinner? Was the steak too rare?"

"Dinner—and the steak—was perfection."

"Then why are you avoiding me?"

"I'm sorry." It wasn't a reflexive apology; Eve truly meant it. She hadn't considered Callum's feelings in her desire to put some distance between them. "I just... I just wonder if maybe it's best if we give this some time. Some space maybe?"

"Why?"

"Honestly?" Eve hesitated, not sure how he'd receive her reasons for wanting space.

"That's preferable, yes."

"Your mom."

"My mom?"

"She hates me."

"She doesn't hate you."

Eve simply raised her eyebrows in response.

"Okay, maybe you aren't her favorite person, but hate is a strong word."

"Did *I* do something?" For all of her overthinking, Eve couldn't for the life of her imagine how she'd managed to land on the wrong side of Mama McT.

"Not at all. She's just being weird and overprotective. It'll pass."

Eve frowned. "I'm not used to people not liking me."

"What I like best about you is how humble you are." He chuckled and went to kiss her forehead, but she stepped back, her frown deepening.

"I didn't mean it like that." She crossed her arms protectively around herself.

"Eve, honey, I was just teasing." A new awkwardness stretched between them.

"It's okay. But maybe we should slow things down a bit. Maybe just until the ice thaws toward me."

"Do *you* want to slow things down a bit?" he asked. "I mean, if my mother had not shown up, would you be slowing things down right now?"

"No." She didn't hesitate. "But she did show up, and she does have strong feelings on the matter, and that changes things."

"I'm a grown man. My mom doesn't get to choose who I date. I'm honestly a little pissed at her for how she's acting."

"You're right, she doesn't get to choose that. But I don't have a family to stick their nose in. Nobody cares who I date. And to be honest, it's a lonely place to be. I don't want to be the one responsible for breaking your family apart."

"No, that would be my mom. Not you." Frustration was thick in his voice.

"I appreciate you saying that. Truly. But it still doesn't sit well with me. All I'm asking for is some time to let the dust settle. Let's just go slow, is all."

Callum regarded her silently for a moment. "You do realize all I want to do is scoop you up, take you home, and have my way with you. You bring out my inner caveman."

A smile tugged at the corner of her lips. "As appealing as that sounds, you'll have to curb your neanderthal urges. For now."

"I will try. For you. For now."

"Thank you."

"*Now* can I kiss you?"

"Now you can kiss me." She stood on tiptoe and leaned in, a trill of pleasure rushing through her when his lips brushed hers.

The kiss was over all-too-quickly and he left her alone with her bottle of wine and her sushi roll. She enjoyed both in her window seat overlooking the street below, people watching and savoring her meal. Then she curled up with a book and immersed herself in a whole new world, one without disapproving mothers or unsettling feelings.

Eve had told Callum she wanted to take things slowly, but it seemed easier to her to simply avoid him altogether. He wasn't the only one with primitive urges whenever they were together. She didn't trust herself to have any sense at all where he was concerned.

Avoiding him meant avoiding the Kelpies and dinner invitations. It was easy enough during the day because when she'd broached the topic of Splash In with Moira, her boss had praised her initiative and put her in charge of creating the displays and coordinating with cross-promotions with other stores on the strip. That gave her plenty to keep her mind off all things McTavish.

But in the evenings, Eve found herself eating her meals alone on her perch overlooking the street. Three days in and she'd dubbed herself the Boo Radley of Lakeport.

So, when a text came in from Corinne inviting her to go hiking the next day, she accepted. Surely Corinne wouldn't bring her mom along to that, too. Eve missed her friend and needed a day away from the store and her apartment.

The next morning, Eve scrounged through her dresser for her khaki capris—they seemed the most sensible thing in her wardrobe for hiking. A t-shirt and a pair of canvas shoes and she called it good. She even put her hair in a ponytail, impressed with her practicality.

Corinne, however, took one look at her and shook her head. "There is so much about this that concerns me. But do you at least have hiking boots?"

"Why on earth would I have hiking boots?" Eve countered.

Corinne opened her mouth to respond but apparently

thought better of it. Instead, she told Eve to grab her wallet and keys, they were going shopping.

As they passed the boutique, Eve thought of her promise to return during regular business hours. "Would they have hiking boots?"

"I don't shop there." Corinne steered Eve toward a shoe store over on 7th. Eve told her what size and then left the shopping up to Corinne, who obviously had strong opinions on the topic. Once she was properly shod, Eve followed her friend to her old Ford F-150. The truck looked like it was older than both women, but Eve didn't know cars well enough to know if that was the actual case. Still, it had character, she supposed. And the bright blue and white striped vehicle seemed fitting for Corinne, being both pragmatic and fun.

They swung by the Kelpies to pick up Sadie, who was practically vibrating with excitement when they got there.

"She knows what the harness means," Corinne explained, taking the leash from Ian and kissing him on the cheek.

"Take care of my dog," he called after them.

"Our dog," she corrected.

"Whatever."

Eve took the exchange in with a measure of amusement, breathing a sigh of relief when they were back on the road again without running into Callum or Mama McT.

"So, I'm going on a limb and assuming you've never been hiking before," Corinne broached the topic once they were underway.

"What makes you say that?" Eve teased.

"Just a hunch. I'm a little concerned my usual trail might be a bit much, so I was thinking—"

"No, let's do it. Wherever you usually go is fine." Eve was feeling determined.

"Are you sure? It's like, a six-hour hike."

"Absolutely."

"Okay." The tone in Corinne's voice made Eve wonder what she'd gotten herself into.

That hesitation was reinforced when they parked at the trailhead and Corinne set about getting them ready. She attached water bottles, a collapsible bowl, and something else Eve couldn't identify to Sadie's harness. Then she shimmied into a pack that made Eve wonder if they were moving out here or just spending the day.

"Can I carry anything?" Eve wasn't heartbroken when the answer was no. As they set out on their hike, she was full of wonder and curiosity. There was so much to see; she didn't want to miss a thing.

Sadie clearly had been hiking before. The dog had waited patiently for Corinne to fit her harness with its gear and didn't require prompting to sit patiently at the edge of the trail to allow others to pass. Any communicating Corinne did with Sadie was through quick sounds that were more like tsks and clucks. The dog was definitely in her element out on these trails; her doggie smile never left her face.

It didn't take long for Eve to feel like her lungs were on fire. Of course, so were her legs. The trail climbed straight up, and she couldn't see an end in sight. She desperately tried to breathe normally, not wanting Corinne to know how much she was struggling. No wonder the woman could pack away donuts like nobody's business. She scaled mountains for fun.

Eve thanked her lucky stars when Sadie stopped to relieve herself. She pretended to look out over the landscape, but really, she was just trying to gasp for air without Corinne seeing. After the dog was done, Corinne scooped it up in a bag and tied the bag to Sadie's harness.

"We pack in, pack out," Corinne explained. "Leave nothing but footsteps behind. And there is no way I'm carrying that bag the rest of the day. She did it, she can carry it."

"She's a cold, hard woman, isn't she, Sadie-girl?" Eve commiserated with the dog, who seemed unperturbed by her new cargo. The more Eve was around Sadie, the more the idea of a dog appealed to her.

When Corinne finally declared it time to stop, Eve nearly wept with relief. Her legs were vibrating they were so exhausted. Corinne prepared them a picnic spot and Eve gratefully accepted the chance to sit down—and was even more grateful to accept the bottle of water her friend handed her.

They sat in silence, drinking their water, nibbling on beef jerky, and looking out over the mountain. The breeze brushed their skin, soft as any caress.

"So, are you going to avoid my brother forever?" Corinne finally asked the question Eve had been expecting all day.

"I explained to him—"

"All of the reasons you want to take it slow," Corinne interrupted. "But I think he's sad you've disappeared altogether."

"That was not my intent." Eve frowned. "I just need some time. I guess I was hoping your mother would kind of forget about me. Or leave."

Corinne laughed outright. "I've wished for that many times myself."

"Don't get me wrong, she's great. Everybody loves her. She's just—"

"A lot," Corinne finished for her. "I know. But she'll get over herself. You have to trust our family is strong enough to withstand one tiny girl from Louisiana."

"That's just it—I don't know what your family can or can't withstand, and I don't want to be the one responsible for breaking it up."

"Do you like Callum?"

Eve smiled reflexively. "Very much."

"Then trust that. Give it a chance. Men who make you smile like that don't come along every day. Don't waste it."

Corinne wasn't wrong. Eve knew that. Still, she changed the subject. "What about you? Any guys catch your interest?"

Corinne laughed. "I've known all of these guys since high

school. If they haven't managed to woo me by now, it's not happening."

"What about tourists?"

"The boys of summer never stick around." She shook her head briefly but then smiled. "They sure are fun while they're here, though. All right. Enough of that. We'd better head out if I'm going to be home before the check-in rush."

"This is my punishment for turning the conversation on you, isn't it?" Eve moaned, stretching out her protesting muscles.

"Take heart, the hard part's done. It's downhill on the way back," Corinne promised.

"Downhill. I like the sound of that."

They were almost halfway back when Eve heard a sound she didn't like. She knew very little of snakes, but the rustling sound accompanied by a large gray and black snake in her path set off warning bells—she'd never seen a rattlesnake up close and had no desire to tangle with one now. Eve let out an expletive and jumped off the trail, looking wildly from the snake to Corinne, completely at a loss for what to do next.

"That's a gopher snake," Corinne told her, the corner of her lip twitching. "You can see by the shape of its head. And you're standing in poison oak now."

"What? I am?" Eve wanted to hop back out of it but didn't trust herself not to find something even more treacherous. "What do I do?"

"I'd recommend getting back on the trail."

"Is it safe?"

"Yep. Look, he's already moving on."

"He rattled," Eve tried to explain her reaction.

"They do move their tail like a rattlesnake, but that's just so the rustling grass will make you think they're something they're not."

Eve scowled. "Sneaky little buggers."

At that, Corinne did laugh. "You might want to get a shower when you get home. Get the oil from the poison oak off you as soon as you can. And put your clothes straight in the wash."

"I will most definitely be getting a shower as soon as I get home." *Getting a shower and retreating to the safety of a book,* Eve mentally amended. She couldn't for the life of her fathom why people did this sort of thing on purpose, and she'd most definitely had enough adventure to last her for a while.

CHAPTER 8

At first, Eve thought she'd dodged the poison oak bullet. Two days after her ill-fated hike, she discovered she was wrong when a swath of angry blisters appeared on the back of her calves, just above where her boots ended.

Even with oatmeal baths and slathering cortisone cream on the rash, she still wanted to crawl out of her own skin. While she had zero inclination to ever go hiking again, she did swing by the store to buy a pair of long pants that the clerk assured her would be good for hiking, just in case.

And, since she was close, she stopped by the coffee truck to grab herself a latte and a pastry.

"Oh, hey, that's a nasty-looking rash," a voice behind her said.

Eve turned to see Martha in line. "Yeah. Went hiking with Corinne and got in some poison oak."

"You really should wear long pants on the trail."

"So I've learned." Eve did her best to let it go at that.

"Are you settling in okay? You like our little town?"

"I do," Eve replied, glancing up to see if it was her turn yet. "It's a great little town. Everyone's so nice."

"Well, not everyone, from what I hear."

Eve's confusion must have been evident because Martha plunged ahead.

"Don't you let that Sorcha McTavish scare you off of her youngest son. You just make her nervous because anyone with enough moxie to move across the country on a coin toss will give her a run for her money, and she's used to being the queen bee."

There was that word again—moxie. The people of Lakeport must be pulling from the same dictionary; she'd heard it more since moving here than she had her entire life up to this point. She didn't have the faintest clue how to respond to Martha's revelation, which made her all the more grateful when it was her turn at the counter.

She got her breakfast, cringing when the guy said, "Enjoy your breakfast" and she responded with "You, too!"

She told herself Martha hadn't heard that as she said goodbye to the woman, though the amusement on Martha's face said otherwise. Eve then proceeded to spend no small portion of her walk home wondering if everyone in town knew how she'd come to be here. And she wondered if Martha was right, was her move the reason Mama McT didn't like her? If so, what could she do about it?

When Eve got back to her apartment, there was a new chair on her stoop. While not quite as large as the last one, it wasn't a small chair. The thought of wrestling it through the door without spilling her coffee was not an appealing one, so Eve shrugged and settled into the chair long enough to eat her breakfast. Luckily, she always had a book in her purse, so she was quickly engrossed in the world created by the author. So much so, she didn't bother to move inside even after her food was done.

And that was exactly how Callum found her: curled up in a chair of unknown origin on her front stoop, reading.

"Um… hello," he greeted her.

"Hi." She looked up at him and smiled.

"Do I want to know what this is?"

"The furniture fairy came again."

"Furniture fairy?"

"Well, someone keeps dropping furniture off and nobody seems keen on taking credit for their act of kindness, so… furniture fairy."

"Makes total sense." He put his hands in his pockets and leaned against the wall. "And do I want to know why you're using it in the hallway? Does it not fit through the door?"

"Maybe. I don't know. I haven't tried it yet."

He blinked at her, either unsure how to respond or waiting for more explanation.

"My hands were full when I got home, so I sat down to read while I ate my breakfast. And then I was comfortable and didn't feel like moving it."

He cracked a grin. "Would you like help?"

"Sure. I haven't injured you lately. Sounds fun."

"Only my heart."

Eve rolled her eyes. "Oh, wow. Ouch. Do guilt trips often work for you as pick-up lines?"

"I don't know. I was trying something new there. Did it work?"

"I'm not feeling it."

"Damn."

"But get the chair inside and I'm willing to reevaluate." She patted his arm consolingly.

"At your service."

"Thanks."

"But you will have to get off of it first," he reminded her.

"Good help is so hard to find," she teased, even as she gathered her things and climbed over the chair to open the door and set her stuff down inside the apartment.

"Isn't it, though?" he quipped, even as he began flipping the chair on its side.

After much struggling and swearing, the chair was inside and in its new spot in the living area. Callum flopped down in it and heaved a sigh. "That thing was heavier than it looked."

"All teasing aside, I'm glad you came along. The last one was a total bear to get in here by myself."

"You could have called. I would have helped."

She smiled but shook her head. "I do not need to call you every time I face an obstacle."

"Maybe not, but you could. I'd come."

Eve sank onto the room's other chair, regarding him for a moment before responding. "That was a much better line."

"Well good. Because I came over to see if you want to go to the drive-in with me tonight."

"You have a drive-in?" Eve couldn't contain her excitement. "I have never been to a drive-in."

"They're showing a double feature, if you're game."

"I am absolutely game. What time?"

Callum seemed pleased at her response. "I'll be here at seven so we can grab a bite beforehand."

"Do I need to bring anything?"

"Nope, just you." He stood back up. "And now, I'd better go before you put me to work again or something."

"Wouldn't dream of it." They both knew she was lying.

Eve had a short shift at work that day, so she used her free time after to swing by the furniture store to ask if they knew who'd bought the chair.

"Hey, Larry," she greeted the affable owner with what she hoped was her most charming smile.

"Why hello there, young lady." Larry's return greeting was both friendly and straight out of Mayberry. "What can I do for you today?"

"This might sound weird, but I'm hoping you can help me

with something—" Eve took a deep breath before diving into her explanation of the mysterious furniture that had begun appearing on her doorstep. "Since the most recent chair looks suspiciously like one that I saw in your window, I was wondering if you could maybe help me out a bit."

"You have a good eye. That chair did come from here. Do you like it?"

"I love it," she enthused. "But I'd like to thank whoever gave it to me."

"That's awfully considerate of you. I wish I could help."

"Larry, I had you pegged as the type of guy who knows all of your customers. Surely you remember who bought it."

He gathered his full height, his body language telegraphing his offense. "Of course I remember."

"Wonderful!"

"But I can't tell you."

She deflated. "Why not?"

"It wouldn't be right." He shook his head. "If they wanted you to know, they'd tell you."

Oh sure, now someone cares about confidentiality, Eve grumbled to herself. But when *she* was the topic of conversation, everybody was a gabby goose. She held her tongue, knowing she was just being petty.

"I'm sorry, dear."

"That's okay. Thanks anyway."

Still slightly surly from hitting a dead end with the mystery of the furniture fairy, Eve stopped by the boutique for some retail therapy.

"Ooh, another date?" Jenna asked by way of greeting.

"Yep. I need something cute to wear to the drive-in."

Jenna hopped off her perch behind the counter. "On it."

Twenty minutes later, Eve was headed home with a pair of boyfriend jeans, a white crop top, and some super cute strappy heels.

Callum picked her up right at seven, greeting her with a low whistle. "Eve, you are stunning."

"I'm in jeans." She blushed.

"My assessment stands." He held his arm out to her. "Does Mexican sound okay for dinner?"

She accepted the offered arm. "That sounds amazing."

He took her to a place with a patio on the lake where they ordered raspberry margaritas and tacos. The food was good, the conversation easy, and time flew by. Eve would have sat and whiled away the evening there, but he was soon ushering them on to their next stop. The first movie of the evening was an action-adventure flick she had little interest in. The second was a '90s classic.

But the movies themselves didn't matter; it was the experience she was there for. He backed into the space and opened up the back of the Jeep, revealing a cozy little nest he'd made for them. The back seats were gone, in their place, a pile of blankets and pillows.

There was no graceful way to clamber into her spot, so Eve kicked off her shoes and tossed them in the back before giving up on being graceful and just climbing in. The pallet was surprisingly comfortable. She curled up next to Callum's side and couldn't help noting how nicely she fit and how good he smelled. She tried to focus on the movie, but the combination of comfy bed, full belly, and margarita was enough to knock her out. Next thing she knew, he was nudging her awake.

"I hate to do this because you look so peaceful, but they're kicking us out."

"What?" Eve lifted her head, confused.

"You fell asleep."

"Oh shoot. Sorry." Eve struggled to clear the fog from her brain. "Was the movie good?"

"Not bad." He sat up and stretched his arms. "Watching you sleep was better."

"You're smooth when you want to be, Callum McTavish."

"I like to think so." He leaned over to give her a quick kiss before climbing out of the Jeep and turning to offer her a hand.

Eve remembered belatedly that she didn't have shoes on. She tried to play it off as no big deal but wasn't sure she pulled it off as she hobbled around to the passenger door. When they got back to her place, he walked her to her door, gave her a kiss that left her dizzy, and told her to sleep sweet.

If she was being totally honest, Eve had to admit that she paid very little attention to her job the next day. She dusted the same spot twelve times and thought about Callum with a goofy grin on her face. That was pretty much all she accomplished. When her shift was over, desperate for some Corinne time, she made a beeline for the Shattered Kelpie.

Corinne was checking in a customer, a pretty brunette who looked to be about their age. She was wearing an adorable outfit that looked like something straight out of the 1940s and had an air of confidence about her that Eve admired—and maybe even envied a little.

When Eve would have stepped back into the shadows to wait, Corinne called out in greeting. "Eve! Hey, I'm dying to talk to you. Get over here."

"I can wait."

"No, I want you to meet Nora. Nora Jones. She just checked in; she'll be staying with us for the next week."

"Like the singer," Eve observed before she could think better of it.

"But without the 'h,'" Nora amended. "I'm just Nora with an 'a.'"

"Nice to meet you Nora with an 'a.'" Eve nodded, still not sure where most people stood on handshakes these days.

"Nice to meet you, too, Eve." Nora's smile was warm and knowing. Eve liked her immediately.

"So, you went out with Callum last night, huh?" Corinne abandoned all desk clerk duties and leaned forward conspiratorially.

"How did you know? What did Callum say?" Eve hoped he hadn't instantly gone to his sister bemoaning the fact that his date had fallen asleep. *Did that officially make her the worst date on the planet?* she wondered.

"Oh no, I heard this from Mama McT... seems she found some super cute heels in the back of my brother's Jeep. And, you know, a bed." Corinne was barely containing her amusement.

Eve paled. "No. Please tell me you are joking."

"I'm sorry to intrude, but I believe I need some details here." Nora leaned into the conversation.

"I've gone on a couple of dates with Corinne's brother, but their mother hates me because I moved across the country on a coin toss," Eve summarized.

"You and I need to talk," Nora informed her. "Because I'm here trying to make a decision about a major cross-country move."

"Yeah? From where to where?" Corinne asked.

"San Francisco to St. Augustine, Florida."

"Why St. Augustine?" Corinne asked. "Just curious. I know nothing about the place."

"Oh, it's cool," Eve interjected. "The oldest city in America. Totally haunted. Neat old buildings."

"Haunted?" Nora raised an eyebrow.

"Oh yeah. I did one of the ghost tours when I was there. It was unreal. Definitely check out the Casablanca Inn. I swear you can see the old lady still floating around those halls." Eve surprised them both with her enthusiasm.

"I can't say I've ever had an inclination toward the paranormal, but I imagine the history of the place would be fascinating," Nora said.

Corinne shook her head. "That's going to be a hard pass from me. I think I'd wet myself if I saw a ghost."

"Speaking of wetting oneself, I left straight from work in San Francisco. I should probably get checked in." Nora straightened.

"Oh, yeah, sorry." Corinne guiltily handed her a key and her driver's license back. "But I still want to hear why St. Augustine. We should grab dinner while you're here."

Nora smiled at each of them. "I'd like that. Shall we say the pub next door at eight?"

"Oh no, Eve might want to steer clear of the pub for a few days, at least until things blow over with Mama. How do you feel about Thai food?"

Plans were made and the women went their separate ways for the afternoon. Eve tried to spend her free time walking, but everywhere she went, someone wanted the scoop on why her shoes were in Callum's Jeep. It was a disheartening realization that living in the city might have been more crowded, but it had offered her a privacy that she'd taken for granted. With the exception of one or two nosy neighbors, people had kept to themselves, and she'd moved through life with a certain anonymity.

Here, she seemed to be the entertainment for the day, and it was too much for her introverted, awkward spirit to process. So, when Callum texted to check in, she knew she had to be honest with him: Her first inclination of wanting to take it slowly had been the right one. She just needed a few days to think and let it all settle down a bit.

Eve worried she'd hurt him, but she also figured he could use the time to rein in his mother. Besides, if they got serious, she'd be dodging the daggers coming from Mama McT for the rest of her life. It was not a pleasant prospect.

Out of the corner of her eye, Eve noticed Martha headed her way with a look of determination on her face. Eve pretended not to notice, instead doing a U-turn and heading back to the safety of her loft. Reading until dinner seemed the better option at this point.

Later, when she was sitting at the restaurant with her two new friends, enjoying good food, great wine, and plenty of laughter, the downsides of living in a small town felt worth it.

"Okay, okay, okay... let me get this straight," Nora began.

"You have a 'furniture fairy' who is mysteriously leaving furniture on your front stoop, and you have no idea who it is?"

"Right," Eve confirmed.

"Did you try asking the furniture store who bought the pieces in question?" Nora asked.

"He was no help."

"Interesting—" Nora seemed to be mulling over the possibilities.

"Maybe they want to remain anonymous," Corinne suggested.

Eve turned a pointed gaze to her friend. "Is it you?"

"Do you really think I could lug all of that furniture up those stairs?"

"That's not a no, and you have two brothers who do whatever you tell them to."

"Not everything I tell them to," Corinne lamented. "If they did, their love lives would be in much better shape."

"I love a good mystery," Nora announced. "I'm going to help you figure out who your fairy is."

Eve liked the sound of that. "Ooh, this will be fun."

"I'd much rather hear about St. Augustine," Corinne changed the subject. "What's this big decision you have to make?"

"Oh, that." Nora's shoulders fell, as if feeling the weight of her decision anew.

"That doesn't sound good," Corinne observed.

Nora took a sip of her wine before plunging into her story. "I inherited a bookstore from an uncle I've never even met."

"I've always wanted to inherit something from a long-lost uncle," Eve mused before realizing she'd said that out loud. "Oh, sorry. Go on."

"He was my mother's brother. They haven't spoken since the '80s. She never would tell me what their falling out was over; she won't even talk about him at all."

"How sad." Concern creased Corrine's brow. Eve imagined she must be thinking about her own brothers.

"I always thought so. I have a big family on my dad's side, but just Uncle Walter on my mom's side. According to her, I didn't miss much by not meeting him, but I'm not so sure I trust her assessment of the matter. She seems fairly biased." Nora sighed and picked at her food. "Anyway, he passed away suddenly. A heart attack, they think. His attorney reached out to me to let me know that I'd been named the sole heir."

"Oh wow." Eve thought Nora must be facing a myriad of emotions right now. She knew she would be.

"Apparently there's all kinds of legal hoops and whatnot before the estate can be settled, but he wanted me to know what my uncle's wishes were so I would have time to think. Assuming no creditors step forward or nobody else says they have a claim to the store, then it would be transferred over to me."

"That's crazy. Do you want it?" Corinne asked.

"I have an amazing job. Moving to Florida was never even kind of on my radar." Nora shook her head, then paused. "But, on the other hand, running a bookstore sounds pretty cool. And it would be a chance to get to know my uncle in some way, my last chance, really."

"Is it possible to go down to check it out before making your decision?" Corinne asked.

"It is—the attorney did ask if I'd be interested in keeping the place going while they sorted things out. But, and this is a big but, that means taking a leave of absence from my job. I work in such a cutthroat office; I worry taking time off could completely derail my career. How did you make your decision, Eve?"

"I flipped a coin."

"Oh, I thought you were joking about that."

"No, sorry. That actually was my strategy."

"Oh my. That certainly took some—" Nora paused, seeming to search for the word.

"Moxie?" Eve supplied.

Nora shook her head. "I was thinking more along the lines of a special level of 'I'm so done with this.'"

"That works, too," Eve conceded. She hadn't even realized it at the time, but that's exactly where she'd been. As she listened to the laughter floating around her, she had to admit that maybe her choice had been risky, but when you can see no way forward, anything that gets your feet moving again isn't all bad. Even if it's flipping a coin.

CHAPTER 9

*A*s expected, it wasn't too many days before Corinne was after Eve to give hiking one more try. "It's fun—and the odds of running into a snake again are incredibly small. I swear you'll like it once you get the hang of it."

"I think we have differing definitions of fun." Eve gave Corinne the side-eye. She suspected it had less to do with the joys of hiking and more to do with Corinne looking for ways to hang out while still avoiding her mother. "But I will come with you. Just give me a few minutes to change."

This time when Corinne picked her up, Eve was prepared, wearing both her long pants and her hiking boots. She even had her own water bottle.

Still, by the time she was halfway up the mountain, Eve was having the epiphany that skinny wasn't necessarily the same as healthy, and she should perhaps look into doing some form of cardio on a regular basis. But then she thought about her books and how much she wanted to be curled up in her window right now and set the thought of intentionally exercising aside. After all, why look a gift horse in the mouth?

She was so wrapped up in her thoughts that she didn't hear the sound until Corinne threw an arm out to stop her. Then she heard it—and she instantly knew the difference between the rustling grass of a gopher snake and the true rattle of a rattlesnake. Like the one she was hearing now. The two women stood frozen, staring at the coiled snake in their path. Eve had thought he was a stick on the trail until he'd pulled himself into striking position.

"What do we do?" she whispered, just as Sadie decided to take care of it by placing herself in between the women and the snake. The movement caused the snake to strike. Sadie yelped, recoiling in pain before lunging forward to give chase. Corinne snagged the handle on the dog's harness, pulling her back away from the retreating serpent and somehow landing both women and the dog in a pile on the ground.

Sadie whined, startling them both out of their shock.

Corinne shifted to examine the dog. "Oh my goodness, baby, are you okay?"

"There. Puncture wounds." Eve pointed to the dog's front leg.

"Okay." Corinne shimmied out of the pack on her back without letting go of the dog. "We need to pour some water over the wound."

Eve grabbed her water bottle and complied. "Is that good? What else can I do?"

"There's a red harness in my backpack. With two big, black straps. Grab it."

"Got it. What now?"

"See if you can slide it on. That part goes on the neck. Yeah, and that goes around the back." Corinne motioned with her head. "Good. Now help me get her up. The strap goes around me like this. Yeah. Help lift her."

Eve did her best to comply with the instructions as they hoisted the 75-pound dog up. Corinne shifted her body to absorb the new weight, taking a deep breath before looking to Eve. "Can you grab my pack?"

"Absolutely." Eve hadn't realized how much additional

weight Corinne had been carrying each trip. No wonder she was able to hoist the dog with such ease. "Good Lord, Corinne. What do you have in here?"

"Lunch. First aid kit. A battery pack. A bit of survival gear in case we ever get stuck…" Corinne continued to name off the list and Eve realized there was more to true hiking than she'd realized. Perhaps she was better off just sticking to sedate trails in parks or something.

The walk back down the mountain felt like it took forever. Eventually, the women were working together to hoist the dog into the cab of the truck. Eve climbed in, pulling Sadie closer to her so Corinne had room to drive, marveling at the animal's calm.

Even though it was technically Ian's dog, Eve found herself calling Callum. She explained what happened and he promised to meet them at the vet, hanging up before she had a chance to clarify if he knew where to go.

"The vet's number is in my phone." Corinne tossed her phone to Eve. "Can you call them and tell them we're coming in? She was bit by a Pacific rattlesnake. They'll need to know what kind of antivenom to give her."

Eve nodded, doing as she was told. It didn't take long for them to get to the clinic. Callum's Jeep was in the parking lot already, though. She braced herself for him to be angry or terse; her father would have been filled with an icy rage over something like this. Instead, Callum greeted her with a hug, asking if she and Corinne were okay. Once he was assured of their safety, he turned his attention to the dog, who licked his forehead while he tried to scoop her out of the seat. She continued kissing his forehead as he carried her inside with Eve opening doors for him. Corinne had already darted inside to get them checked in.

She waited in the lobby rather than overcrowd the exam room. It was killing her not knowing how things were going, though. Logically, she knew it wasn't her fault. Still, some part of her thought maybe she was bad luck on hikes. Two hikes, two snakes. To her, that seemed like a sign from the universe that hiking was not her thing.

Just as she was beginning to wonder what good she was doing sitting out here and if she should just walk home rather than be in the way, Corinne reemerged.

"How is she?" Eve rose to meet her friend.

"Okay, I think." Corinne nodded. "The vet thinks we got her here in time. He's giving her some pain medicine now and then we can take her home. We have to watch her closely for the next forty-eight hours and keep the bite from getting infected, but she should heal. If it had been her face or chest, it might have been a different story. But it was her leg, and we got her here quickly, so… she's a lucky pup."

Eve wasn't sure if she'd go so far as to say lucky, but she was relieved to hear Sadie was expected to recover.

Callum appeared, carrying the newly bandaged retriever. "Hey, Eve, can you get the door to my Jeep for me?"

She moved to do as asked, surprised when he asked if she'd mind riding back with him to keep an eye on the dog. They rode in silence for a couple of minutes, but it didn't last.

"Are you sure you're okay?" Callum glanced at her in the review mirror. "It didn't get you?"

"No, Sadie jumped in between us and the snake. As soon as it bit her, it took off."

"She's a good dog." He was silent for a moment before asking, "And has my mom been okay? She hasn't done anything I should know about or anything?"

"I haven't seen her."

"I'm sorry Eve. I swear she's not normally like this."

Not quite sure what to say to that, Eve sat silently stroking the dog's head.

"If it had to happen, I'm glad you were with Corinne. I don't think she could have gotten Sadie out of there alone."

"I don't know," Eve disagreed. "Corinne is the strongest

woman I know—mentally and physically. If anybody could do it, she could."

"I suppose you're not wrong. Still, I'm glad Corinne has you. She seems happier since you came to town."

"Good. She makes me happy, too." Eve liked knowing that her presence had had a positive impact on Corinne.

"For the record, I'm happier since you came to town, too." He met her eyes in the rearview mirror one last time before letting the subject drop.

When they got back to the Mortal Kelpie, Eve opened doors as instructed so Callum could carry Sadie up to Ian's apartment above the bar. Callum made himself at home, getting a bed and supplies situated for Sadie. Eve mostly just sat with the dog unless Callum gave her directions.

Ian's apartment was as different from Callum's house as their personalities. Where Callum's place was tidy and modestly decorated, Ian's was cluttered and full of interesting memorabilia, including a large sign that read, "Equal Rights for Women."

"Don't get the wrong idea," Callum must have noticed the direction of her gaze. "He's not especially forward-thinking. He stole that from the prop room back in high school."

"So, he's had that thing for twenty years?" Eve clarified.

Callum chuckled. "Pretty much, yeah."

"Interesting." Eve continued to survey the room. It told a story of a life well lived, or at very least a life full of experiences. Pictures, edges curling, tacked to a bulletin board. Ian and unknown people from all over the world. Ian surfing. Ian holding a koala bear. Ian hanging off the edge of a cliff. "Actually, where is Ian today? I'm surprised he didn't meet us at the vet."

"He's at a conference in the city. He wasn't due back until tomorrow, but I think he's driving back in tonight after it's over."

"Oh, I hate that he's cutting his trip short."

"I'm sure she'll reschedule." Callum's tone was wry.

"Is conference code for something?"

"No, he did have a conference," Callum explained. "But I suspect there's a woman, too. Either that, or he's taken a sudden keen interest in the restaurant industry."

"Well, he does own a restaurant."

"That never occurred to him before."

"Perhaps he's smart, looking for love in a city two hours away. That might be a safe distance from your mother."

"Yoo-hoo," the mother in question called from the door.

Eve froze, mortified. She looked at Callum and mouthed, "Did she hear me?"

He shrugged, looking entirely too amused for Eve's liking, before calling out to his mom. "We're in here, getting Sadie settled."

"Poor pup." Angus was the first to join them in the living room, Sorcha having made a beeline for the kitchen. "I hear she's had quite a day. Oh, hello Eve. I hear you've had quite a day, too."

"Not one I'd like to relive any time soon," she admitted before smiling up at him. "Hello, sir. It's good to see you again."

"Gah, enough with the 'sir' talk. I told you, call me Angus."

"It's good to see you again, *Angus*," she corrected.

"It's good to see you, too—and in one piece."

"Yeah, I think I've had enough hiking to last me a while. Last time, I got poison oak. This time, the snake. I need a boring hobby."

"Try kayaking," he advised. "It's not boring, but if you're on the lake, it's nice and calm. Relaxing."

"I'll do that." She took his advice to heart.

"Oh, hello, Eve." Sorcha's tone was much cooler than her husband's when she made her appearance.

"Hello, ma'am." Eve nodded once, noticing the other woman didn't bother to correct her.

"How's the patient?" Mama McT asked, not bothering with pleasantries, either.

"Well, I think. She seems happy to be home," Eve answered. Sadie corroborated by thumping her tail.

"What did the doctor say?" Angus asked.

"That she'll be okay. We just need to keep a close eye on her for the next forty-eight hours. We can ease up a bit after that, but if she gets an infection, we're supposed to take her back in right away." Callum reached down to scratch the dog's ears before taking a seat on the floor next to Eve.

"I've put together a schedule for us," Corinne announced her presence. Eve hadn't even seen her come in.

Callum grinned at his twin sister. "I figured you would."

Corinne ignored her brother's teasing. "Eve and I need to take tonight off to recover from our trauma, so Mama & Pop, please sit with Sadie tonight until Ian gets home? Callum, I need you in the bar tonight, so can you take tomorrow morning? Eve, you get off work at three tomorrow, right? Can you head over then?"

"Absolutely." Eve nodded, glad to help.

"I'm sure we can cover it," Mama McT protested. "You don't have to bother Eve."

"It's not a bother at all," Eve assured her even as Callum spoke up.

"Are you kidding? I've been trying to figure out how to get Eve back in the bar. I appreciate Sadie taking one for the team."

Eve rolled her eyes and blushed, looking over at Callum as if to say, "Really?"

He winked and tapped the end of her nose lightly, a gesture that was equal parts endearing and irritating.

"If I'm no longer needed, I think I'll head home." Eve had visions of takeout and a bubble bath, followed by curling up with a good book. *Say what you will about the outdoors being great, books don't bite*, she mentally proclaimed.

"I'll walk you." Callum started to get up, too.

"No, that's okay. You hang out with your family." Eve could tell her words disappointed him, so she softened them by bending down and kissing his cheek. "Maybe we can grab dinner this week or something."

"I'd like that." The look he gave her made her want to melt in a puddle at his feet. She said awkward goodbyes to the rest of the room and hightailed it home, stopping only long enough to pick up some Chinese food. As she waited for her meal, the thought occurred to her that she should probably cook on occasion. But the truth was, she hated cooking and it didn't seem worth the effort when it was just her. She wondered if Callum expected her to be a good cook or if he'd care since he clearly was.

Her evening was every bit as relaxing as she'd hoped it would be. The only problem was that it passed too quickly, and she found herself at work long before she was ready. Her mood wasn't helped by the fact that more than one person had heard about the incident on the trail the day before and wanted a firsthand account from her. She suspected some, like Gale Peterson, came by specifically for that reason. And, of course, to deliver a helping of unwanted advice.

"You have to be more aware than that on the trail. Always look where you're going," the woman lectured. Eve smiled and nodded, mentally choking on her response.

"Oh, come off it," Martha joined the conversation. "When was the last time you've spent any time outside, let alone on a trail?"

Eve mouthed, "Thank you" to the woman.

Gale narrowed her eyes at Martha. "It's just good, common sense."

Eve gritted her teeth. "It is, but happily, I will not be on a trail any time soon, so hopefully I won't need the advice."

Martha clucked her tongue. "Oh, honey, don't let that little ol' snake scare you off."

"Hiking was never my thing anyway," Eve assured her. "So, Gale, did you decide on the writing desk? Do you want me to have Callum deliver that to you tomorrow?"

She could have kicked herself the instant the name was out of her mouth because Gale took it as an invitation to start pumping her for information about the shoe drama. This time, Martha wasn't so inclined to save her—she wanted the latest scoop, too. Eve had to admit she was proud of how skillfully she ducked the topic, instead throwing poor Molly under the bus by asking, "Did you hear Crazy Molly is seeing Andy?"

Gale paused mid-question and eyed Eve. "Which one?"

"Big Andy, not Little Andy," Eve replied.

"Is it serious?" Martha asked.

Eve shrugged. "Can't say, but Jenna saw them all snuggled up at the café last night."

The women exchanged a knowing glance, making Eve wonder what she didn't know about Big Andy. Still, she got them out of the shop without the conversation veering into uncomfortable areas again, making Eve think maybe she was starting to get the hang of this small-town thing. She was so proud she even texted Callum to let him know her victory, to which he assured her he was very proud that she'd learned to use gossip as a defensive weapon.

When her shift was over, she spent a few minutes visiting with Lily before heading over to the Kelpie. Her stomach rumbled, reminding her that she hadn't eaten yet. She popped by the bar long enough to snag a hug and a drink from Ian before trudging up the stairs for puppy duty.

Corinne greeted her with a friendly hello but was already late for her shift at the inn, so there was no time to chat. Eve was quickly left alone with Sadie, who seemed to not be faring so well. The dog barely lifted her head to say hello, her tail thumping out a mild greeting. Eve had intended to read, but it seemed the dog needed a friendly voice, so she sat with Sadie's head on her lap, stroking her ears and talking softly to her.

She told the dog about her home in New Orleans. She talked about her mom and her neighbors and the dusty little shop she'd loved. She told Sadie she'd never had a pet before, but she wanted one—just as soon as she remembered to get permission from Moira. Sadie whined and pressed closer to Eve.

"Oh, you poor, sweet girl. I wish I could take your pain away," Eve soothed.

A voice from the door startled her. "You're very good with her."

Eve looked up to see Mama McT standing there with a basket of fish and chips. "I didn't see you come in."

"Ian wanted me to bring you some dinner. He said you probably forgot to eat lunch again."

"Thank you." Eve smiled. "He's not wrong."

When Eve started to get up, Mama McT shooed her back down. "No, no. You two look comfortable. I'll bring it to you."

"Thank you," Eve said again.

"I think Sadie likes you as much as my children do," the older woman observed.

"I like them all very much, too." Eve meant it. They'd made her world a bigger, brighter place by being in it.

"So, what happens if small-town life wears thin?" Mama McT asked. "Do you flip another coin and move on?"

"I lived in New Orleans thirty-two years. Over the last two years of my life, I've lost everything that tethered me to the place. I think it was a justifiable change." Eve surprised herself with her steady self-defense. She didn't even trip over the words.

Sorcha nodded as if considering, but let it drop. "Well, your food is getting cold. I can leave you to it."

"Please tell Ian thank you for me."

"I'll do that. Have a good night, Eve."

"You have a good night, too, Sorcha."

Left alone in the room she looked from the door down to Sadie. "What do you know, girl? Looks like there might be hope yet. Think I can win her over?"

The dog whined and sighed. Despite Sadie's cynicism, Eve held hope in her heart.

CHAPTER 10

It took her a couple of days to work up to it, but Eve did text Callum as promised, asking if he'd like to go to dinner sometime. He responded with a suggestion that they go fishing on her next day off. She couldn't help remembering the family that had set her on her journey, so she agreed with no small measure of excitement.

Not wanting to repeat the hiking fiasco, she went to the Mortal Kelpie at lunch in search of Ian.

She met his cheerful greeting by getting straight to the point, "I need to borrow fishing gear."

"I would do anything for you, Eve—"

"Thank you!"

"—except loan you my fishing gear. A man does not loan out his fishing gear."

Eve frowned at him, unsure where to go from there.

"But—I will take you shopping."

Eve was left with little choice but to accept. He did offer her a delicious plate of salmon for lunch, so she forgave him.

"How's Sadie?" Eve asked around forkfuls.

Ian frowned. "Not great, unfortunately. If she's not improving by tomorrow, I'm going to take her back in."

"That poor thing. I wish there were more I could do for her."

"She enjoys your visits."

"I'll be back for another after my shift is over," Eve promised.

"Nah, I'll ask Pop to take your shift. You and I have shopping to do," he reminded her with a wink.

"Right. How could I forget our shopping trip?"

Eve finished up her lunch and blew Ian a kiss on her way out the door. She was almost late clocking back in at work because Jenna stopped her on her way by.

"Hey, Eve, you gotta swing by before Splash In. We got some darling fall tops in that would look amazing on you."

"Yeah, well, let's see how my bank account looks after Ian McTavish takes me shopping for fishing gear. He had a mischievous gleam in his eye I don't quite trust."

"Ian McTavish?" Jenna faltered and then chuckled. "You're right not to trust the mischief in that man's eyes."

Eve smiled and waved at her friend, making it back to work just in the nick of time. They were less than a week away from the seaplane festival, so Eve and Moira spent most of their afternoon going over the cross-promotions Eve had lined up for them.

Ian showed up about fifteen minutes before her shift was over, leaning against the counter and chattering her ear off while she tried to reconcile her drawer. It took three tries to balance it with the distractions, but Eve suspected that was his intent, and telling him to be quiet would only reward him.

And then they were off, headed to the tackle shop to appropriately prepare Eve for her first-ever fishing trip. She wanted the small purple pole that looked about her speed, but he insisted on a large black pole with a spinning reel that looked way too complicated, despite his assurances otherwise. He started handing her items off the shelves, her arms quickly filling with waders, a tackle box, hooks, sinkers, fishing line, pliers, lures... when he plopped the iconic fishing hat on her head, she called a halt to it.

"Ian, I can't afford all of this."

"Nonsense, it's my treat."

"It feels like a bit much. I may not even like fishing. What if I never go again?"

"Of course you'll go fishing again. Wasn't that the whole reason you moved here?"

"Not exactly." Eve wasn't sure how to explain the difference to him, so she dropped it. "Can I at least set some of it down at the register?"

"Oh, all right." He took pity on her, helping her get everything over to the counter.

By the time he was done, the dollar amount on the register made her eyes water. They were both loaded down with bags on the walk back to his green Subaru Outback. The first time she'd seen his car, she'd said, "Please tell me you named him Oscar."

His reply had been "I didn't realize it was an option to *not* name him Oscar."

"Some people don't name their cars," Eve had reminded him.

"Monsters, all," he'd concluded.

They grabbed some dinner on their way back to her place. She liked hanging out with Ian because he didn't try to talk to her about Callum or his mother. He told her about the girl in San Francisco, that she was pretty and smart, but things just weren't clicking. She wanted him to move to the city, but he was happy with his life at the Kelpies. They talked about what she could expect from Splash In, and he warned her that she needed to start thinking of a Halloween costume now because there would be revelry.

When it was all said and done, Eve was pretty sure hanging out with Ian had set tongues to wagging anew and her living room was full of crap she was positive she'd never use, but it had been a delightful evening in all, and she went to bed happier than she had in a while.

She woke up bright and early the next day, determined to be ready when Callum arrived. She felt ridiculous in the enormous overalls, boots, and hat. Her tackle box was packed, and her rod propped by the door. Her suspicion that the outfit was overkill was confirmed when Callum took one look at her and doubled over laughing.

"Let me guess? Ian helped you prepare?" he asked once he caught his breath again.

Eve narrowed her eyes, unamused by the McTavish brothers. "I'll just go change. Be back in a minute."

Muttering about overgrown adolescents all the while, Eve went and changed into hiking pants and boots. The t-shirt was the one piece of the original outfit she kept.

"Oh, now, please put the hat back on. It was adorable," Callum pleaded when she reemerged.

Eve eyed him for a moment before relenting and retrieving the hat from her bathroom floor. She spent the entire drive back to the Kelpies plotting how to get back at Ian. Unfortunately, she wasn't particularly creative in that regard. She made a mental note to ask Nora her opinion; she seemed the clever sort.

Once they were at the lake, she was so busy helping Callum get the canoe in the lake and loaded that she was forced to set aside her irritation. He held the canoe for her to clamber in, shoving it off from the shore before hopping in himself.

It took a few tries for her to get the hang of paddling, but she soon got it. After a couple of wobbly goes and a bit of laughter, they found their rhythm and were able to simply enjoy water quietly lapping at the oars as they sliced through the still glass. Eve loved the way it felt when the canoe surged forward both confidently and peacefully.

"You're awfully quiet," Callum observed.

"Just enjoying the moment. This is nice."

"I think Pop's right—you'd like kayaking."

"I think I would."

"You can always use the Kelpie's kayaks. I'll get you a key."

"Thank you." Eve was excited at the prospect of being able to spend more time out on the water. It was immensely calming.

"If it helps at all, Ian did choose a good rod and reel for you."

"It's good to know the trip wasn't a total waste."

It took them a while to get to the spot Callum had in mind for fishing, but Eve didn't mind. She was enjoying the ride so much that she'd have been happy if that's all they did. Still, she had moved halfway across the country to live somewhere that she could someday teach her children to fish—and she had the gear—so she listened patiently as Callum taught her how to cast using the spinning reel.

Her first attempt, she dropped the line behind her instead of casting forward. The second attempt took Callum's hat off. By the third go, she managed to successfully release the line at the right instant for a good cast.

It took all of ten minutes for the new to wear off and for her to get bored with fishing. Still, she enjoyed listening to Callum share stories from his childhood. She laughed, picturing the time their boat broke down at the opposite end of the lake and Angus had to walk the shoreline towing the boat while his children pretended to be mighty explorers. The picture he painted was one she wanted for her own children someday, making her happy all over again that of all the places she could have ended up, she had chosen this place.

"Oh!" Eve straightened excitedly. "I felt a tug."

"You've got a nibble," he told her. "When he tugs again, you tug back. Not too hard… that's it. Now reel."

With a bit of laughter and a whole lot of luck, Eve was soon proudly holding the line containing her first fish over the boat.

"That's a nice-looking bass. Now, to get him off the line—" Callum started, only to be interrupted by a very excited Eve.

"I know this one." She grabbed the fish just the way she'd seen the mother do the month before. Thankfully, the hook came out easily enough. She wasn't sure what she'd have done if it had resisted at all. She leaned over, careful not to tip the boat, giving the fish a second to orient before loosening her grip. He swam away, slowly at first, before darting into deeper waters.

"I am impressed."

"I'm just glad he hadn't swallowed the hook or something."

"Fair enough. Need help with your line or anything?"

"Nope, I'm good, thanks," Eve responded, laying her pole back down in the boat.

"Oh, are you done already?" he asked, surprised.

"I felt kind of bad for the fish," she admitted. "I think I'll just watch."

His response to that was a deep, rich laughter. "It's a little early for lunch, but we can head that way if you want?"

"Oh, I'm fine with whatever. I'm enjoying being on the water."

"Want to explore a bit?"

"We can fish if you want, for real."

"Nah, come on." He tucked his gear away and picked up his oars. "I'll show you my favorite spots."

"I'd like that."

The water trail he took her on had them hopping from small island to small island through the narrows, with him pointing out various waterfowl and Native American dugouts along the way. He told her the history of each point of interest. Sometimes, they'd just glide along silently, absorbing the majesty of the mountain mirrored perfectly in the lake.

There weren't any public access points along the trail, so they ate lunch in the canoe. Eve rather liked it, though. It took them the entire day to make the whole circuit and then paddle back to the Kelpie's boat launch. Eve could tell already that her muscles would be protesting by the next day.

He dropped her off at her apartment before heading home to clean up, promising to be back to pick her up for part two of their date at nine. Eve had to admit she was curious as to what he had planned, although the focus of her curiosity shifted when she got to the top of her steps to find a kitchen table with a note pinned to it:

The table's not from me. But I do know who your furniture fairy is.

xo Nora

Tired as she was, Eve grabbed a quick shower and threw on fresh clothes before heading over to the inn to see if Nora was around. The front desk clerk said she was at the pub, so Eve headed over. She was eager for news on Sadie, anyway.

Turns out Angus was covering the bar for Ian, who was still at the vet with Sadie. "They're not sure they can save the leg," he told her.

"Oh, wow. I'm so glad Ian took her in when he did."

"He's feeling bad he didn't take her sooner."

"It's always so hard to know what to do in these situations." Eve felt bad for Ian. She felt even worse for Sadie. She wished she could rewind time and not go on that stupid hike. "Keep me posted, okay?"

"Will do," he promised, handing her the glass of wine she'd ordered.

"Thank you, kind sir."

"You're welcome. I'll have that sandwich out to you in a bit."

She held the glass up in salute to him before heading toward Nora and sliding into the chair across from her uninvited.

"Oh good, you got my note." Nora brightened at the sight of Eve.

"I did. And I am impressed. You work fast."

Nora shrugged modestly. "Just a bit of sleuthing. And a little stakeout. No big deal."

"So, what did you find?" Eve leaned in, dying of curiosity.

"It started with Callum. But then Ian found out and brought the TV stand. Then Martha caught wind of it and had Callum pick up a chair she no longer needed. It spiraled from there. Someone named Crazy Molly donated a dresser. Moira bought you the chair from the furniture store. The table came from a gentleman named Albert who runs one of the boat docks."

"Oh wow." Eve wasn't sure how to process that. She wondered if she should be embarrassed, but mostly she was just incredibly grateful. And, more than anything, she felt welcomed.

"Right? How adorable is that? The entire town is in on it now. You're going to have furniture coming out of your ears by the time they're done."

"Huh. That's—amazing."

"Yeah, it is," Nora agreed. Conversation paused as Angus brought Eve her meal. She thanked him and then turned her attention back to Nora.

"Have you decided what you're going to do about St. Augustine?"

Nora nodded thoughtfully. "I believe I have. I'm going to take a leave at work to go check it out. If nothing else, see the place, talk to his employees and friends. I'd like to know more about Uncle Walter if I can."

"I think that's a good call," Eve said. "Jobs come and go, but this chance won't come again. You'll kick yourself if you don't take it."

"That was my thinking."

"But I want updates."

Callum materialized at the side of her table, placing Eve's sandwich in front of her. "Fancy meeting you here."

"Hello, handsome." Eve's smile was genuine. She'd just spent the day with him, and yet she was still inordinately happy to see him. "Care to join us?"

He looked to both women. "Do you mind?"

"Not at all." Nora gestured at the seat next to Eve.

"Oh, where are my manners?" Eve realized with a start Callum and Nora hadn't met. "Nora with an "a," this is Callum. Callum, this is Nora."

"It's a pleasure to meet you Nora with an 'a.'"

"And you as well," Nora replied, amused.

"Couldn't get enough of us McTavishes?" Callum turned his attention to Eve.

"I'm stalking you," she teased back.

He settled his arm over her shoulders. "That's what I thought."

Conversation flowed easily between the three of them, with Callum stealing bites of Eve's sandwich when she didn't eat it fast enough.

"You know, I bet your dad would make you one, too, if you asked," she observed.

"He wouldn't. He'd tell me to go make it myself."

"Ah. I see your problem." She couldn't help smiling at him. He was so darned cute. Her smile was stilled by the sight of Mama McT, frowning sternly and marching toward them.

"We tried to reach you." She came to a stop in front of Callum.

"I talked to Ian. He said there was nothing I could do there."

"Corrine came by on her way home," Mama McT added.

Callum's scowl was fierce. "Well, I asked the surgeon and he said they were good, they didn't need me to scrub up, so I didn't see the need to crowd the waiting room at the animal hospital."

His mother opened her mouth to respond but he held up a hand.

"Mom, I am sorry about Sadie, and I will most definitely be in the rotation helping with her when she comes home, but can we please not do this right now?"

"Fine." The woman's body language said she was anything but fine. She turned to Nora, nodded her head slightly and said, "Lovely to meet you," before striding off.

Nora blinked, looking from Callum to Eve. "What just happened?"

"My mother." Callum ran a hand through his hair in frustration. "My mother just happened."

"His mom isn't my biggest fan," Eve explained. "It makes her a little—" she paused, searching for the word.

"Crazy," he supplied. "She is acting certifiably insane."

"I was going to say testy," Eve amended. "And the family dog is injured—she had to have emergency surgery today—and now I think everyone's just a little on edge."

"That was very diplomatic of you," he complimented.

"You probably need to go sort that out," Eve said. "We can do the second half of our date another night."

"Not a chance." Callum shook his head. "The meteor shower is tonight. I'll go talk to Mom, smooth things over. Let's meet at my place like we planned."

Eve nodded and accepted the kiss he placed on her head as he got up to go. Goodbyes were said and then Nora and Eve were left alone.

"Okay, so—" Nora took a bite of a French fry and regarded Eve. "Now that he's gone, what's the real story?"

"Oh my goodness, that woman *hates* me." The words came out in a tumble. "I like Callum so much, but I just don't know that I can deal with always being in the middle of a drama."

Nora was nonplussed. "Sure you can, if you love him."

"Who said anything about love?" Eve was flustered.

"The two of you did, with the way you were looking at each other just now. Total adoration."

"I've only known him a month."

"Is there a prescribed timeline for these things?"

"It feels like it should be longer than a month."

Nora shrugged in response.

"What about you?" Eve asked. "I didn't even think about it before when we were discussing if you should move. Do you have a significant other who'll want you to stay in San Francisco?"

Nora's eyes took on a sadness that was tangible. "I was in love once, but that was long ago. I don't know that I could make room in my heart for anyone else."

"Oh. I'm sorry." Eve desperately wanted to ask what happened.

"He died," Nora answered the question Eve had been afraid to ask. "In a rock climbing accident. I lost him and his dog. Tank. A pit bull. Solid muscle but the biggest marshmallow you'll ever meet. Kind of like Aaron was."

"There's nothing I can say that even comes close to helpful."

Eve's heart broke for her new friend.

"It's okay." Nora brightened, though the smile didn't reach her eyes. "It was eons ago. But it's possibly what tipped the scales in favor of moving. San Francisco was our town. I'm not sure I'll ever be able to let him go as long as I stay."

Eve impulsively reached out to grab Nora's hand, taking the woman by surprise. "You are going to love St. Augustine. It's a beautiful city full of history and things to explore."

"Thanks." Nora patted Eve's hand awkwardly. "So, have you decided what you're going to do about your furniture fairy, or should I say fairies?"

"I don't know for sure, but I'd like to do some little something while still respecting their anonymity." Eve thought for a moment. "I mean, Moira's easy. I know what she likes. But some of the others, I don't even know who they are, let alone what they like. But I'd like to figure out some random act of kindness."

"I can help," Nora offered.

"You're going to be busy enough with your move."

"Nah, I love this kind of stuff. Let me see what I can find out for you."

"Sure, thanks," Eve conceded. Nora was right, Eve would get a lot further along with her help.

"Good, that's settled. Now tell me more about this van life thing…" Nora changed the subject.

"Well, I don't know much. I never did it—it was just an option pre-coin flip."

"Still, it intrigues me."

Before long, the women were saying their goodbyes and exchanging phone numbers so they could stay in touch. Nora would be heading home the next day to pack her things in preparation for a new life in Florida. Eve was grateful for having met her. She would miss her new friend, though. And, for the first time, Eve had a sense of what it meant to be a permanent resident in a lake town.

CHAPTER 11

*E*ve knew she needed to get dressed for work, but she didn't want to move just yet. She much preferred to stay piled up in bed, remembering part two of her date with Callum. They'd laid on his roof and watched the meteor shower. The sky had looked like something from a movie: thousands of stars had been splashed across the sky, twirling and twinkling their promise that this universe was so much more infinite than any human can comprehend.

They made a wish on the first streak of light to trace a path across the sky.

"What did you wish?" he had asked.

"Nuh-uh. I can't tell you. It won't come true."

"Is that a thing?"

Eve thought for a moment. "I think so."

"Come to think of it, is wishing on a meteor the same as a falling star?"

"I don't know, is it?"

"I feel like I should know the answer to this," he said.

"Yeah, me, too. But I don't." Eve had sighed and snuggled closer to Callum, her eyes greedily drinking in Milky Way above. "This is nice."

"It is."

"I appreciate you taking things slow. Giving me time to process."

He squeezed her tighter. "You're worth the wait."

"That. It's things like that that scare me. Well, that and your mom."

"Why?" He shifted so he could see her better.

"My last boyfriend was a narcissist." The words just sort of tumbled out. "I know the word gets tossed around a lot these days. But he truly was. Textbook. And until you've lived with a narcissist, you can't begin to comprehend how that messes with your head."

He had seemed afraid to speak, afraid the wrong word from him would silence her.

"The narcissist thrives on making you think you're crazy. But they start off so charming. It feels so perfect. It's not until you're in too deep to save yourself that you start to notice the red flags. And you, Callum McTavish, have been incredibly charming. Well, once you stopped being such a jerk, that is."

"Gee, thanks."

"You could have easily swept me off my feet if I'd let you. I just, I just needed to be sure I could trust you were what you seemed, I guess."

"That's fair," he conceded. "And somewhat of a relief. I thought it was just my mom acting so crazy keeping us apart."

"That does not help."

Now, as she prepared to pull herself out of bed, Eve sighed, the memory of the evening still warming her from the inside out. For the first time since meeting Callum, it had been more than reacting to the rush of being around him and the flutter she felt in her stomach whenever he came to mind. It had felt like the beginning of something real. After her admission, he'd just held her close and pointed out constellations.

With a smile, Eve stretched and pried herself out of bed to get ready for work. She'd lingered too long for breakfast and looked longingly at her coffee pot on her way by to see if she had any laundry clean.

Moira greeted her with a knowing smile. "You look awfully happy."

"I am," Eve admitted.

"I knew that youngest McTavish would grow on you."

"For once, I will gladly admit to being wrong."

The McTavish in question materialized in the doorway. "I come bearing coffee and news of Sadie."

"I welcome both." Eve reached out for the coffee, planting a kiss on Callum's cheek as she did. "Well, I suppose I only welcome the news if it's good."

"It is. She came through the night well. If all goes well, they might even let her come home this afternoon."

"That's so fast!" Moira exclaimed.

"Right?" Callum turned to his aunt. "But the vet said she meets most of the requirements for them to feel confident she'll do well at home. They've got her on antibiotics, and they said she'd go home with a pain patch."

"Oh, I hope he gets to bring her home." Eve couldn't imagine how worried both Ian and Corinne must be.

"Doc Mullins said the first few weeks would be the worst, but most dogs adjust fairly quickly."

The bell above the door tinkled, interrupting the conversation. Eve instantly recognized Two-Timing Bill and had the passing thought that she'd never pegged him as the antiquing sort.

"Hey, Bill," Callum greeted the man before turning back to Moira and Eve. "I'd better let you ladies get to work. Catch you later."

"Hello, Bill," Moira greeted him cheerfully. "What can we help you with today?"

"I, uh—" he looked down at his feet briefly before forging on. "I was wondering if you have any tables, but like little ones. For a hallway or something. I need something to throw all my crap on when I walk through the door."

Moira's smile deepened. "We do have a couple of console tables around here somewhere. Let me show you."

He started to follow but then paused, looking back at Eve. "I was wondering if maybe Eve could show me?"

Eve and Moira exchanged a glance. Eve had never so much as said hello to the man—if for no other reason than out of solidarity for Crazy Molly—so she had zero clue why he'd requested her. Telling herself it was just more small-town curiosity over the newcomer, she came around the counter to lead him to the most masculine table she could think of that might work for him.

"Sure thing. I have one in mind for you—let's see what you think of it and go from there."

He followed her back to the table in question, mumbling something she couldn't quite hear.

"I'm sorry, I didn't catch that." She paused and turned.

"I said you look pretty today," he repeated a little louder.

"Oh." Eve was startled. "Thank you. So, um, this is the table…"

It was the most awkward sale she'd ever made, but he did wind up buying the table. As he loaded it in his truck, he asked if she had plans for dinner. She thanked him but told him she had a date already. She couldn't be sure, but he looked like he suddenly regretted buying the table. She almost felt bad for him but knowing what he'd done to Molly kept her from quite reaching that threshold.

"That was incredibly odd," Eve told Moira as she reentered the store.

The afternoon moved on, and while it seemed there were more male customers than normal, Eve told herself she was imagining things. When she ran the deposit down to the bank for Moira, she was waylaid by George from the hardware store.

She hadn't been lying to Bill, she did have a date after work

—with a brown-eyed blonde who happened to have three legs. After clocking out, Eve scurried down to Ian's for her turn to Sadie-sit. Not even a desire to avoid Mama McT could keep her from checking on the dog for herself.

On her way through the bar, she was stopped by one of the servers. She vaguely recalled him having waited on her before. She couldn't for the life of her imagine why he felt the need to stop her and get the details on her day just now, though. Eve tried to politely extricate herself, but he wasn't getting the hint and she really needed to get upstairs to relieve Corinne, so she had to interrupt him a little more bluntly than she was used to.

"I'm so sorry I'm late," she announced as she rushed into the apartment. "One of the waiters... I forgot his name... something with an 'N'..."

"Norris?"

"Yes! Norris. He was oddly determined to talk to me for some reason. Actually, a lot of men have been oddly determined to talk to me today." Now that Eve stopped and thought about it, the men of Lakeport had been especially attentive all day long.

Corinne sighed heavily before standing to stretch her back. "I can solve that one for you."

"What's that?"

"The mystery of why the men are all so chatty today—that's my mother's doing. I believe she's taken it upon herself to find you a more suitable match than her son."

"I just can't even begin to decide what to do with that information."

"Yeah, I got nothing. I swear this is not the mother I know and love. I'm beginning to think aliens have invaded or something."

"Yes, that's the most plausible explanation, surely." Eve wondered what Callum would think of his mother's latest antics but set it aside for now. Corinne needed to get to work. "So, Sadie. How's she doing? Anything I should know?"

Corinne walked Eve through the instructions and told her to text Ian or the vet's on-call number should anything go wrong.

"Oh, and we're going to the winery Thursday."

"*The* winery? Aren't we kind of in wine country?" Eve asked. "Surely there's more than one nearby."

"Henshall's, you smart aleck." Corinne rolled her eyes. "Clearly you've been spending too much time with my brothers and not nearly enough with me."

"Clearly." Eve smiled. "The winery it is. Text me details. I'll be there."

Eve was fairly certain she needed something new to wear to the winery, so the next day during her lunch hour, she popped by to say hey to Jenna and browse the fall shirts as promised.

"So, this Norris guy. He is tenacious, I'll give him that."

"Oh yeah?" Jenna held out a purplish-blue top for Eve to try.

"Yeah. He brought by a cup of coffee and a gas station flower this morning. He was there right when the shop opened."

"That sounds sweet."

Eve stopped browsing and looked at Jenna. "Maybe I just need to set him up with someone else, divert his attention elsewhere."

"Nope." Jenna shook her head. "Don't be looking at me. I don't date men. Married one once; it was a horrible mistake I don't see myself repeating. Besides, I'm currently in an incredibly committed relationship at the moment. With myself."

The women continued to joke as they poured through the racks, pulling out anything that caught their eye before whittling the pile back down as Eve tried on the various clothes and modeled them for Jenna. She nearly made herself late back from lunch, but she was successful in finding a new outfit for the winery.

Eve stashed her bag under the counter at work just as

another random man stopped in with a sudden urge to shop for antiques. She'd be irritated with Mama McT, but she'd had a great week for sales. So much so that she was on track to earn a bonus, which she fully intended to use to book a weekend in the city for her and Callum. She hadn't told him that yet, though. She was waiting to see if the money materialized first. But the irony of his mother's ploy funding a romantic getaway with him amused her. Greatly.

While she was mildly dreading an afternoon dodging arrows from Callum's mom, she was looking forward to seeing not only him, but also Ian and Corinne. After much cajoling from his sister, Ian had hired a sitter for Sadie, and everyone had their shifts covered at work so the entire clan could be there. A prospect that made Eve both nervous and excited.

When they arrived at the picturesque winery, nestled in the mountains overlooking the lake, it took Eve about point-two seconds to realize why Ian had balked at the outing. Clearly, he and the pretty blonde who greeted their party had a past. One that wasn't entirely in the past.

As she linked arms with Corinne, walking arm and arm toward their table on the covered patio, she leaned over and whispered. "You're either evil or a genius. I can't decide which."

"What on earth do you mean?" Corinne batted her eyelashes innocently.

"You chose this place to mess with your brother."

"Or right a wrong," Corinne amended.

"I need to hear this story." Eve studied the pretty blonde curiously. With big blue eyes, fashionable clothes, and immaculately styled hair with not a flyaway or broken end to be seen, the woman was classy. Classier than Eve could ever hope to be, not that she was losing much sleep over it.

No sooner than they took their seats, Mama McT went tripping after the blonde, who Eve learned was named Virginia Henshall. Angus and Ian went to order their snacks and wine, leaving Eve, Callum, and Corinne at the table.

"Okay, somebody spill it, quick."

"They were engaged," Corinne told her. "But she broke it off."

"It looks like your mother approved of the match," Eve observed, watching Mama McT practically simper over Virginia.

"The Henshalls are old money, well respected in town. Mama was over the moon when the engagement was announced."

"What happened?" Eve asked.

"I don't think her family was quite as enthused," Corinne speculated. "I suspect they had something to do with her change of heart."

"Better to find out before the wedding than after." It was Callum's first contribution to the conversation. Something about his tone left Eve wondering if he was speaking from some level of experience. She made a note to ask him about it when they were alone.

Ian and Angus returned with several bottles of wine and a plate of assorted cheeses and crackers, effectively ending that particular conversation. From that point on, Angus kept the wine and conversation flowing freely. It was easy to see where Ian got his charisma, even if he was more subdued than usual today. From the looks she caught him sending Virginia's way when he thought nobody was looking, it wasn't too hard to guess why. The normally vibrant man was putting off more "kicked puppy" vibes than anything at the moment.

It felt so good to be surrounded by family and warmth and laughter that Eve made the conscious decision to set aside her irritation with Mama McT to simply enjoy the day. Unfortunately, the woman didn't seem inclined to just let things rest for the day.

"Eve, honey, it seems you're quite popular lately," Mama McT turned the conversation her direction, causing Eve's stomach to lurch. "Anyone in particular catching your eye these days?"

"You mean, other than my boyfriend, Callum? Not particularly, no." They hadn't decided on a label yet, but the words were out of Eve's mouth before she could stop them. She didn't have time to worry that he'd take exception to her statement because he took her hand on the table in a public display of support that warmed her heart.

"I didn't realize you two were exclusive." The other woman bristled.

"We are," Callum answered.

"I, um, I would actually really appreciate it if you could help us get the word out that I'm not interested in Norris, Bill, or anyone else right now." Eve mustered every ounce of courage she could to voice the request. She didn't come right out and accuse Mama McT of turning the horde loose on her, but the implication was there that she knew, and it was enough to turn the woman's voice to ice.

"I can't imagine why you'd need my help with that."

Eve opened her mouth to respond but was interrupted by Callum. "Has anyone tried that goat cheese? The one with sundried tomato? It's so good. We should get some for the pub."

Her shoulders fell as the conversation moved on. She wasn't upset with Callum for diverting the topic—she certainly didn't want to ruin the lovely day—but she was also disheartened that nobody seemed inclined to help her circumvent the unwanted attention. Maybe it wasn't fair to put that on him, but since a McTavish started this mess, it seemed reasonable a McTavish should help end it. Besides, Norris and his band of merry men certainly didn't seem inclined to listen to her and she was dangerously close to losing her temper over the entire mess.

CHAPTER 12

Having grown up in New Orleans, where a festival meant the streets were overflowing with people from all over the globe, Eve was slightly amused at the difference between Mama McT's description of Splash In and the reality of the event. Still, there *was* a certain festivity in the air and Eve had never in her life seen an amphicar before, so the weekend had that going for it.

Despite attending the opening BBQ for the event with Callum on her arm, it didn't slow down any of Eve's potential suitors. She practically growled with frustration when she couldn't get a plate of pulled pork without Norris trying to turn it into a moment between them. Callum's amusement over the situation did nothing to endear him to her.

"What?" he asked defensively when she scowled in response to his laughter. "It's sweet."

"It's not sweet. It makes me uncomfortable, and she set that poor man up to be hurt unnecessarily. Geez, I can't even walk down the street without somebody flirting right now."

"I would imagine most women would be delighted to have that problem." He seemed to be truly struggling to understand.

"Says the big, strapping guy." Eve crossed her arms, the

evening all but ruined for her. She had no idea how to explain to him that talking to strangers unexpectedly like that was exhausting for her. Her anxiety had skyrocketed since Sorcha McTavish started with her shenanigans. "I think I'm going to go over there for a while. I don't want to have this conversation right now."

"Over where?"

"Not here."

"Oh."

Eve left him gaping at her retreating back. Perhaps it was petulant, but she was beginning to lose patience with him, his mother, and the entire situation. Determined to put the whole thing behind her, she found the first safe group she could and inserted herself in that conversation.

"Hey, Jenna! How goes it?"

Jenna brightened when she saw Eve. "Hey, girl. Come meet my friend, Andrew Leighton. He's an Alaskan bush pilot in town for the weekend."

"Oh, wow. That must be incredibly cool. Nice to meet you, Andrew."

"You know what? It is incredibly cool," he agreed, offering up a charming grin. Eve couldn't help noticing he was a handsome man with golden hair, tanned skin, and a bit of scruff covering an angled jaw. "And it's nice to meet you, too, Eve."

Out of the corner of her eye, Eve saw Norris headed their way, so she shifted to place herself in between Andrew and Jenna.

"You're using us as human shields, aren't you?" Jenna accurately surmised.

"Absolutely."

Andrew looked at the two women. "Now I'm curious."

"See that guy over there?" Jenna nodded in Norris's direction. "He's not so good at picking up social cues and Eve is too nice to be brutally blunt."

"Ah. Well, I'm happy to be of service, then."

"Thank you." Eve felt relief wash over her when Norris scanned the room for her and then gave up, having lost her in the crowd. She was pretty content to hang out in between the two of them, listening to their conversation and eating her pulled pork. So much so, that it took her a minute to realize when Andrew was talking to her.

"Can I convince you to take a ride in my plane tomorrow?"

"Is that a euphemism for something?" It had been a long week of awkward double entendres—most of which were a complete stretch.

"No." He laughed. "It's my Cessna C-172 Skyhawk. My seaplane."

"That sounds great, then. Thanks." Eve realized she was actually pretty excited. It was short-lived, though, because she saw Callum striding her way with a terrifying scowl on his face.

When he stopped in front of their group, he spoke not to Eve, but to her friend. "Jenna. I had no idea you'd be here tonight."

"Andrew is an old friend of mine. He invited me."

"I guess I didn't realize you and Eve were friends, either." He finally looked at Eve, his expression almost wounded.

"This is who you're dating?" Jenna asked Eve.

"Yes. And why do I feel like I'm missing an important piece of the puzzle here?" Eve looked from Jenna to Callum.

Callum's voice was filled with ice. "Surely you know already."

"Know what?" Eve struggled not to raise her voice. The man might have nearly a foot on her, but she was getting ready to thump him. He was being impossible tonight, on so many levels.

"Eve, Jenna is my ex-wife."

The words echoed through Eve's head. "Your what? How was I supposed to know she was your ex-wife? I didn't even know you had one of those."

"I should probably excuse myself." Andrew looked like he wanted the earth to swallow him whole.

"No, I'm the one who interrupted you and Jenna when I was

trying to hide from Norris. You stay. I'll go." Eve backed away. "It was lovely to meet you, Andrew. Jenna, I'm sure I'll see you next week. I still need to get a new jacket. I didn't have much use for one back in New Orleans."

"Eve—" Callum followed her, reaching for her hand when she wouldn't slow down or turn around. She pulled it from his grasp and kept walking.

"No, Callum. Not here." She blinked back humiliated tears. Outside, away from the crowd, she stopped and turned to him. "I opened up to you. Was honest with you. Vulnerable with you. And not only did you leave out something pretty big—that you were *married* before—but then you accuse me of—what? What exactly did you think I was playing at by befriending your ex?"

"I don't know. I just—" He didn't finish the sentence.

"You can't think of one logical thing to say, can you?" Eve raised her eyebrows expectantly. "I feel like I've put up with a lot here. I did it because I thought you and I had a chance at something special. But the first chance you get, you think the absolute worst of me. I'm not going to live my life that way, Callum. I can't."

"Eve, I just didn't know what to think when I saw you two. I generally try to avoid Jenna."

"You live in a small town, Callum. I don't think that's entirely feasible."

"I should have told you about her sooner."

"Yes, you should have."

"I just didn't know what to say."

"Eve, I was married before. We're divorced now. Her name is Jenna." Eve supplied the script for him.

"It didn't feel that simple. She nearly destroyed me. It took years to come to terms with her just walking out like that. I didn't think I'd ever let anyone in again, but then you nearly mowed me down with your car."

Eve chuckled at the memory. "If nothing else, I suppose I made an impression." She paused, taking the hand she'd rejected moments ago. "I'm sorry, Callum. I need some time to process this. And the random men stopping me everywhere I go has to end. Your mom being rude to me has to stop. I don't deserve it."

"No, you don't. I'm sorry I didn't deal with it sooner. I guess I was hoping it would blow over."

"Well, it didn't. If I'm in a relationship with someone, I look out for them. I have their back. I want someone who'll do the same for me." Eve took a step back. "I'm going home now, Callum. I think we need a little space for a while."

"Didn't we just do space?" His voice was laced with irritation.

"Goodnight, Callum." Some part of Eve wanted to cry. Hot tears burned the edges of her eyes but refused to fall. She was too mad to weep.

She'd ridden to the event with Callum, a fact she didn't remember until she'd strode away. She wasn't about to go back and search out a ride, so she just walked. It gave her time to think, or more appropriately, to clear her head.

She did wonder how on earth she and Jenna had known each other this long with neither of them realizing the tie they shared. She couldn't be sure what it meant for their blossoming friendship. It felt weird now, but she also didn't want to just ghost Jenna—good friends were hard to come by. She barely knew the woman, but Eve did believe they'd been headed toward being friends. Still, knowing Jenna had walked out on Callum and had broken his heart changed things. Eve was curious to hear the other woman's side. But she had to admit, after seeing the hurt in Callum's eyes, it made Eve wonder if she knew Jenna at all.

After a restless night, Eve rolled out of bed determined to keep Callum at arm's length until she had a chance to process the whole "I was married once and forgot to tell you" thing—and until he dealt with his mother. She was also determined to keep her friendship with Corinne intact, and to that end, she texted to see about breakfast.

Their usual diner was busting at the seams with townies and

tourists alike, so the women opted to try somewhere new. It, too, looked like a throwback to a bygone era with its cafeteria-style chairs and tables. Any doubts Eve had about the place were erased when they set her French toast in front of her.

She hadn't had French toast since she was a little girl; the smell took her instantly back to Saturday mornings, eating breakfast with her mom in front of cartoons.

"I am dying to know what happened," Corinne said after answering Eve's questions about Sadie, unable to hold it in a second longer. "Callum was an absolute bear after you left, and he won't say why. Because heaven forbid we communicate like adults or anything."

Eve closed her eyes, savoring the cinnamon goodness for just a moment before taking a swig of coffee and diving headfirst into recounting the events of the night before.

"I love my brother, but wow. I had no idea you didn't know. I thought it was weird when you wanted to shop in her boutique."

"I just don't know what to make of it all. I mean, it's not like he's still married. I don't want to create drama for the sake of drama, but I feel like he should have said something by now, you know?"

"Yeah, I get it. I'd be ticked off, too," Corinne empathized. "And I'm sorry my mom is being such a cliché. I thought she'd just get over herself. I should have thought about how she was making you feel before now."

"Thanks." Eve appreciated her friend's words. "I think I just want to go take my plane ride and go to work and not think about any of it for a while."

"I get that. I wish I could go with you for the plane ride. I have an early shift today."

The women paid their check and wandered out the door together, pausing before parting ways.

"I think you were right to draw the boundaries that you did,

Eve. Just be careful that boundaries don't become walls. Talk to Callum before this goes on too long."

Eve nodded, not sure what to say. Corinne wasn't wrong, but Eve wasn't ready to talk to him just yet. That felt like a tomorrow thing.

As Corinne headed to work, Eve wandered over to the seaplane festival, intent on taking Andrew up on his offer of a plane ride. His face lit up when he recognized her.

"Eve, hey! I didn't think you'd come."

"Are you regretting your offer?" She was only half joking.

"Not at all. Just pleasantly surprised that you took me up on it."

"Are you kidding? I've been looking forward to this since you brought it up."

"I just wasn't sure, after—" he trailed off awkwardly.

"Sorry things got weird last night." She scrunched her face.

He shrugged nonchalantly. "It happens. Did you and the guy figure things out?"

"I've decided that's a tomorrow problem."

He let it go. "So, are you ready to go up?"

"Absolutely."

"Great. You're going to want these." He handed her some earplugs.

She accepted them with some trepidation, wondering what exactly she was getting herself into. The entire experience was new to her. It was bumpy and the tiniest bit terrifying, but it wasn't long before they were up in the air and her fears were washed away by the beauty unfolding before her. Eve hoped she never grew too accustomed to the beauty of the place. Whether she was on the shorelines, on the water, or soaring above it, every layer of the lake was stunning in its own way.

The ride was over before she was ready. She thanked him profusely as she left, but not before accepting his offer to grab dinner after her shift. She was sure that would be just one more thing to set tongues wagging, but there was a certain amusement to be had in keeping the gossips guessing. Besides, she genuinely liked Andrew; he made her laugh, and his stories of the Alaskan Bush were fascinating.

Eve's shift was a short one, something she was grateful for since she was having a hard time concentrating on much of anything that day. After, she texted Ian to see if he or Sadie needed anything before heading up to her apartment to change.

She met him at the Mexican restaurant with seating overlooking the lake. It wasn't lost on her that the last time she'd been here had been with Callum. Or that she missed him already, after only a day. Ruthlessly shoving all thoughts of him aside, she focused on the person who was with her now, listening as he told her about his family in Montana and how he'd come to be a pilot in Alaska. He regaled her with stories of shuttling tourists, scientists, and hunters to and from places that couldn't be reached by car. Still, when he told her about the time a grizzly raided his camp, she couldn't help thinking of Callum.

When dinner was over, they parted with a warm hug. Tongues might wag over her dinner with Andrew Leighton, but all he'd truly done was convince her she was ruined for any man besides Callum McTavish. She liked Andrew and could see herself being friends with the man, but there hadn't even been a ripple of attraction. Mostly, just a longing for Callum, the man she was trying very hard not to think about.

CHAPTER 13

Splash In passed in a bit of a blur. Eve had barely blinked before Andrew and the other pilots were gone, leaving the little town to settle down until the next festival rolled around. She hadn't heard from Callum since their fight and couldn't be sure if he was respecting her wishes or if he'd written her off altogether.

Either way, Eve didn't mind the time alone. As much as she loved her new home and friends, her introverted spirit was in desperate need of alone time. The apartment felt a bit too quiet, though, so she took Callum up on his offer and helped herself to a kayak.

Some small part of her was afraid she'd get lost if she strayed too far from the dock, so she kept it in sight as she paddled around, getting a feel for the boat and how to steer. There was so much to see and take in. Being on the water, so close to it, made it feel all the more special. Like she was a part of it all instead of just an observer. By the time she made it back to the shore, she was not only feeling much more Zen about life, but she had also come to the realization that she was completely addicted to kayaking.

Over the next couple of weeks, Eve found herself stealing

away to the boats any time she was off work and the weather cooperated. The temperature was dropping, but it didn't deter her from exploring further and further. When she wasn't on the water, she was shopping for kayaks or gear online, building out her wish list, and daydreaming about trips she could take, new places to explore.

Her dinners with the McTavish brood hadn't resumed, but Eve made a point to eat at the Kelpie on Callum's nights off. She missed her friends almost as much as she missed Callum. His absence only served to highlight how used to his presence she'd gotten, how much she looked forward to sharing things with him, and how much she valued his opinion.

True to her word, Nora sent Eve a list of everyone who'd gotten her furniture, along with what act of kindness would make them happiest. Eve had no idea how Nora did it—from an entirely different city while packing her apartment up, no less. She could only assume it was the woman's superpower or something. Armed with her list, Eve used her free time to start implementing Operation Thank You.

She left a bouquet of sunflowers on Moira's desk, along with a box of her favorite Godiva chocolates. For Albert, she spent an afternoon helping him clean up his yard—after convincing him she just happened to be passing by and truly enjoyed yardwork, neither of which was true. Ian's random act of kindness required a trip to the winery. And, rather than look suspicious, Eve snagged herself a bottle of the sparkling wine she'd been such a fan of on her last visit. And some of the goat cheese with sundried tomatoes, reasoning it was for a good cause.

Methodically, she made her way down the list, determined to repay the kindness of each person who'd made her feel welcomed, all the while trying not to think about what would happen when the only person left on the list was Callum.

Sometimes she dreamed about him at night. One dream, in particular, followed her throughout her day. It wasn't anything elaborate; she'd been sitting on his lap, wrapped in his arms, feeling safe, loved. She missed his gruff-yet-gentle nature and his solid presence. She debated calling him at least a dozen times a day but always talked herself out of it.

When she realized she'd let the infamous Halloween party sneak up on her without even thinking about what her costume would be, Eve was forced to shift her attention. She texted Corinne an SOS, her friend replying with the suggestion to be a pirate, offering up a skirt and hat to the cause if Eve could turn up the right blouse.

Knowing full well there was only one shop in town that had even a remote chance of offering a ruffled white off-shoulder top, Eve sucked it up and headed to Jenna's boutique. The poor woman froze like a deer in headlights at the sight of Eve, who smiled and said, "Hi."

Jenna visibly relaxed at the greeting, making Eve wonder if she'd been expecting a daytime talk show style throwdown.

"I need a shirt for a party tonight," Eve explained, moving toward the rack most likely to hold what she was looking for.

"It's good to see you."

"You, too."

"Does Callum know you're here?" Jenna asked.

"I haven't talked to him since Splash In." It hurt Eve's heart to say the words.

"That's too bad." Jenna must have recognized the surprise on Eve's face because she went on to explain. "I like Callum. He's a good man. I know I hurt him, and he didn't deserve it; I'd like to see him happy."

"Why did you?" Eve blurted out. "Hurt him, that is."

"I was young and stupid and trying to be something—someone—that I'm not." There was regret in her voice. "He was collateral damage. After the dust settled, I thought about seeking him out to try to explain, to apologize, but he wanted nothing to do with me and I can't say I blame him, so I respected his wishes."

Eve nodded, trying to absorb what Jenna was saying. She

knew the reality of life is that none of us escape our time on this planet without hurting others, no matter how oblivious we might be to that pain. Knowing Jenna felt true remorse did nothing to erase the pain she'd seen in Callum's eyes, but Eve was in no position to stand in judgment over something the woman had done more than a decade previous. So, she left her response at a nod and held up a cream-colored blouse, asking, "Do you think this looks pirate-y enough?"

Jenna's smile was brilliant. "I do. It's perfect. And look, I have a scarf over here that would make a fabulous sash."

Eve left the shop feeling a million times lighter than she had walking in. If the McTavishes wanted to awkwardly avoid Jenna for the rest of their lives, that was on them. Eve figured life was too short, this town was too small, and friends were too precious a resource to squander.

With that realization, she knew she needed to grow up and stop avoiding Callum, or rather, allowing him to avoid her. Or whatever it was they were doing. The point was, they needed to talk—about all of it.

High school drama aside, Eve was ridiculously excited about the Halloween party. She felt like she'd barely seen Corinne the last couple of weeks. And, if she was being honest, she was more than a little excited about seeing Callum. To that end, she turned on her bounciest playlist and be-bopped her way around the flat while she got ready, belting out "I Wanna Be Sedated" in a completely uncharacteristic fashion.

When the ensemble was complete, Eve stepped back to survey the final outcome in the mirror. She had to admit, she was rocking the pirate thing. The skirt Corinne loaned her was a deep red. It was ruffled and soft, hitching up on one side to reveal her killer boots. It came with a corset, so Eve used the sash Jenna had picked out as a headscarf instead of using it as a belt. After donning her lipstick, she gave herself one last look in the mirror and then headed out the door, bumping into Moira in the parking lot.

Eve took one look at the woman's red trench coat and matching fedora and broke into a grin. "You're Carmen Sandiego, aren't you? That's amazing."

"Thanks! You like it?" Moira did a playful pose reminiscent of the character.

"I love it. Incredibly clever."

"Well, you make a stunning pirate, dear."

"Thanks." Eve looped arms with Moira, taking it for granted they'd be walking to the party together. She spent the first five minutes of their walk working up the nerve to ask the question that had been on her mind for two months now. "Hey Moira..."

"Yes, you can get a dog."

"What? I didn't even ask yet."

"Callum mentioned it to me ages ago. I've just been waiting for you to bring it up. All I ask is nothing too yippy or drooly."

"No yipping or drool." Excitement washed over Eve. "Done and done."

"Were you thinking a puppy, or...?"

"I was kind of thinking a young adult dog. I've noticed lots of one-year-old dogs up for adoption."

"That's because they're holy terrors at that age."

"Oh. My. Well, I can look for something a little older. I mostly want something I can take out on the water with me."

"Oh, I wasn't trying to discourage you. Get lots of chew toys and take him or her to the dog park every day and you'll be fine."

"Okay, good to know." Eve made a mental note. Now that she had permission, she could hardly wait to find her new family member. She almost debated skipping the party to Google pet adoption events but reminded herself this was her best chance to see and fix things with Callum.

"You know, my brother and his wife are planning to leave again just after Thanksgiving."

"Really?" Eve tried not to show her elation.

"They booked a European cruise. They'll be gone until early next year."

"How nice."

Moira laughed. "You're trying so hard to be diplomatic and I love you for it."

"Angus is very kind to me. I'll miss him." Eve would have been content to leave it at that, but Moira wasn't about to let her off that easily.

"What? You won't miss Sorcha, too?" Moira's voice was rife with mischief. "Don't worry. I'm only teasing you. She'll grow on you and you on her. Just give it time."

Eve reminded herself that Moira had been right about Callum growing on her, though she was a bit more skeptical that it would hold true with his mother, and she still didn't see why Mama McT was so beloved around town.

The Mortal Kelpie was already hopping when the women arrived. As had most of the small town, the McTavishes had gone all out on decorating. The place was appropriately creepy with its purple lighting, fog creeping along the floors, and zombies and witches galore.

"Hey, gorgeous." Ian greeted her by lifting her off the ground in a giant hug. "Nice costume."

"Thanks, you, too." She chuckled at his Ron Burgundy costume, made even more amusing because she knew Virginia would be showing up soon as Veronica Corningstone, making it a perfect couple's costume. If that didn't get the pair talking, she didn't know what would. "How's Sadie doing?"

"Surprisingly well. I think I'll let her start hanging out around the Kelpies again soon. She's getting restless being cooped up all day."

"Good. That she's doing well, not that she's restless," Eve amended.

Ian smiled and promised he'd be back with a drink for her in a minute. He didn't ask what she wanted, so she hoped he chose well for her. She couldn't help chuckling as he stubbed his toe, muttering about stupid fog as he hobbled around the bar.

"Oh, wow," Corinne greeted Eve with a more tempered hug than her brother had. "You are smokin' in that costume."

"Thanks." Eve beamed. The compliments were a little unnerving at first, but she decided she could get used to them. "I'm debating dressing like this more often. I feel like I could rule the world—and it's surprisingly comfortable."

"If you do, you'll undo all of Callum's hard work convincing Norris and his merry band of misfits to leave you alone."

"What?"

"Never mind." Corinne waved her off. The gesture had lost all its charm in the last two months. Now, it was simply annoying.

Determined to not let anything dampen her mood, Eve shifted her focus. "You look stunning. That dress is divine. And the color—it's perfection."

"Yeah?" Corinne flushed, looking down at herself. "I was in a Gatsby kind of mood."

"It's working for you."

Callum came out of the backroom, a crate of booze on his shoulder, which kind of perfectly completed his pirate look. Eve's first thought was that he was ridiculously handsome. Her second was to realize they were two halves of a couple's costume, making her giggle.

"You okay?" Corinne gave her the side-eye.

"This is your doing, isn't it?" she asked, nodding in Callum's direction.

Corinne hesitated. "How mad will you be if I say yes?"

Eve laughed even harder. "I'd say great minds think alike."

"How so?"

As if to illustrate her point, Virginia walked through the door in a pink suit straight out of the 1970s. "I might have done a thing," Eve admitted.

"Is that—?" Corinne stopped short, for once at a loss for words.

"Virginia Henshall dressed as Veronica Corningstone? Yes, yes it is."

"Does Ian know?"

Eve looked to the bar, where Ian stood stunned, watching the woman move across the room with enviable grace. "I'd say he's figured it out."

"What did you do?"

"I may have visited the winery," Eve hedged. "And perhaps confided in Virginia about all the trouble I'm having with Mama McT. She was super sweet. Told me that, if I love him, I shouldn't let anyone—not even his mom—stand in my way. And then you could almost see the lightbulb go off."

"Wait, did you just say you love my brother?"

"That's not the point of the story." Eve dodged the answer, thinking Callum should hear it from her before he heard it from his sister.

"That was a risky move." There was admiration in Corinne's voice. "What are you going to do if Ian flips out?"

"I don't know. What will you do if Callum isn't happy to see me?"

"Yeah, I'm not worried about that even a little."

Eve watched Callum set down the crate he was carrying, appreciating the ease of his movements and the way his muscles peeked out from beneath his rolled-up sleeves. He must have felt the weight of her gaze because when he straightened, he turned to find her in the crowd. When he saw her, a grin broke across his face. It felt like a weight had been lifted, and Eve returned the smile with one of her own, her feet moving of their own accord in his direction.

"Um, okay. Bye. Nice talking to you," Corinne called to Eve's retreating back, her voice laced with amusement.

Eve came to stand in front of Callum, looking up at him and drinking in every feature. She'd missed his face. "Hi."

"Hi." He looked down at her. She wondered if he might kiss her; he certainly looked like he wanted to. Personally, it was taking a great deal of restraint to not fling herself into his arms.

"I heard you're the reason I can walk the streets without being hit on again. Thank you."

"Your no should have been enough." He frowned. "But I'm sorry I didn't get involved sooner. Guys can be dumb. They just needed a gentle nudge."

"Gentle nudge." Eve chuckled, not sure she believed that the nudge was entirely gentle.

"I, uh, better get back to work. It's good seeing you, though." Callum didn't move.

"Yeah. It's good seeing you, too. But I don't want to keep you. I know you're busy." Eve didn't move, either. That is, until Ian showed up to grab her by the shoulders and steer her away.

"What did you do?" he demanded once they were alone in the stockroom.

"What?" She blinked innocently.

"Why is Virginia here?"

"I assume because she wanted to see you. She does know this is your place."

"Why? Why does she want to see me? It's been ten years since she broke off our engagement. Why now?"

"Maybe she's grown up."

"What do I do?"

"Say hello," Eve advised. "See what happens from there."

"I can't go through that again."

"Maybe it'll end differently this time." She rested a hand on his arm reassuringly. "And, Ian, you're one of the three strongest people I know. You can do anything, even this."

He nodded but seemed to be too lost in thought to respond.

"I'm going to go back to the party now. You know where to find me if you need me."

As she emerged from the backroom, she realized Ian never got her a drink. He was obviously too flabbergasted to do so now, so she headed toward Callum, who'd taken over tending bar, to order herself a martini.

"Is everything okay?" Concern etched Callum's brow.

"Definitely," she reassured him, her eyes cutting over to where Virginia stood, looking half-ready to flee. "But I should probably go talk to her before she bolts."

"Ah. So you had a hand in that. I was wondering what changed."

"Let's just say your mother's antics might have served some good after all."

"I'm not sure I want you to explain that. I think maybe I do."

"Later." She smiled at him. "I don't want to think about it tonight. Hey, that's not what I ordered."

"I know. But your order was lacking in Halloween spirit. This is a witch's brew. Much better."

Eve eyed the drink suspiciously. "If I don't like it, you're making me the lemon drop."

"Naturally." His smile made her heart do a little flip.

She tentatively took a sip before giving her approval and heading in the direction of Virginia.

"You look darling," Eve said by way of greeting.

"Thanks. So you do."

"You okay?"

"A little nervous, to be honest. I thought I saw Ian earlier, but he's disappeared. Everyone else is avoiding me—I think they're afraid there will be a blowup and they don't want to be caught in the crossfire."

"There won't be a blowup," Eve reassured her. "Ian's just in the stockroom. I'm sure he'll be out in a minute."

"Did you talk to him?"

Eve shrugged, unwilling to lie but not inclined to share anything Ian didn't want to be shared, either. "I'm much more curious about where the McTavish parents are. Standing next to me could be the true danger tonight. I appreciate your bravery."

Virginia linked arms with Eve and blessed her with a brilliant smile. "I will gladly be your defense."

Eve couldn't help thinking it was easy to see why Ian was so enamored with this woman. Everything about her drew people in like moths to a flame.

The witch's brew Callum had handed her wasn't as tasty as the drink she'd ordered, but it wasn't bad, and it packed a punch. Eve could feel the tension ebbing away as she chattered easily with Virginia, Corinne, and a string of random townspeople who wandered in and out. Ian had resumed his place behind the bar. The line was too long for him to even say hi to Virginia, but the couple spent a fair amount of time watching each other from across the room.

Of course, the tension came crashing back when Angus and Sorcha came in. They were greeted by a handful of people, all commenting on how cute their costumes were—the big, bad wolf and Little Red Riding Hood. Eve didn't realize how tense she'd become until Corinne reached out and linked arms with her. Virginia gave her an encouraging smile. Eve forced herself to take a deep breath. There was only so much the woman could do to her, and it was time Eve stopped allowing Mama McT so much control over life.

And then Callum was there, his hand on the small of her back, the two of them laughing and leaning into each other as naturally as if they'd never been apart. Eve knew they needed to talk, but she was also content to put that off for another day. Tonight, they would simply enjoy one another.

His nearness made it a lot easier to ignore any sideways remarks from his mother. Though, in truth, she was pretty toned down compared to their previous encounters. She almost seemed accepting of Eve's presence. Almost. She couldn't be sure if it was because Callum had talked to her or if word had gotten back to Mama McT that Eve was responsible for Virginia's presence at the party. Perhaps even better was that Norris was working but didn't even look Eve's way once that she could tell.

The one time he even came close to her, he lowered his gaze with a quick, "Excuse me, ma'am," making her wonder just what exactly Callum had said to the guy.

Callum could never stay long. Once the line slowed, he and Ian took turns manning the bar so the other could visit. Ian and Virginia never did get time alone, but both seemed content to exist in the same space and sneak longing glances at each other.

When Eve left for the evening, it was as she arrived—on Moira's arm. Callum did, however, give her a lingering hug and a tender if chaste kiss before she left. Eve might have walked home, but she was pretty sure she floated.

CHAPTER 14

The next morning, Eve was sitting alone at her favorite booth in her favorite café, eating her favorite breakfast of hash browns and bacon with a cup of the best coffee she'd ever tasted. In all, she was feeling pretty danged good about life. The chasm between her and Callum had felt so insurmountable just twenty-four hours ago, but now not so much. Now, she felt confident they could sit down just the two of them, well, maybe the two of them and Alba, and sort things out. She could see a way back to good between the two of them.

Her phone pinged, so she set aside her book and picked it up, pleasantly surprised to see it was an update from Nora.

"I did it! I just pulled into sunny Florida. Wish me luck."

"Ah! I'm so excited for you. Keep me posted on how it goes." Eve tapped out a reply, hitting send just as someone joined her at the booth.

"Good morning, Eve," Sorcha McTavish said coolly, motioning for the waitress to bring her a cup of coffee.

"Good morning," Eve replied warily.

"You and my son seemed to be having a nice time at the party last night."

"We were."

Mama McT sat back, allowing the server to pour her coffee. Then she took the time to add cream and sugar, stirring deliberately, giving Eve the impression the woman was choosing her next words carefully. "I'm sorry if my matchmaking efforts made you uncomfortable. I thought it might be helpful if you met new people. Sometimes it can be tough to break out of our bubble and all that."

"Ah, well thank you. I assumed you were trying to steer me away from Callum, to be honest."

Mama McT looked surprised at Eve's bluntness. Surprise gave way to a cool smile. "I suppose I was. But he's told me in no uncertain terms my help was unwelcome."

Eve wasn't sure how to respond to that, so she just took another sip of her coffee and toyed with her hash browns.

The older woman took the silence as her opportunity to press on. "I've agreed to stay out of it from now on, but you have to know I don't think you're right for Callum. I was hoping I could talk to you, woman to woman, and ask you to please let him find someone who's, well, more suitable."

Eve sighed, her perfect morning gone, along with her patience. "I'm curious—did you ever read *Pride and Prejudice*?"

"Why?"

"Because this little move didn't work out so great for Darcy's aunt. I'm wondering how you envisioned this conversation would go."

"Did you really just compare me to Lady Catherine? That uptight old bat?"

Eve merely raised her eyebrows and took a sip of coffee.

"Look, Eve, I don't dislike you. I see why my son is so enamored with you. I do. But he's already had his heart broken once; I can't sit by and watch it happen again."

"Ian had his heart broken and you're tripping over yourself trying to get her back in his life. Besides, what makes you so sure I'll hurt Callum?"

"You moved cross-country on a coin toss. You have nothing

tying you here. What's to stop you from moving again?"

"Your son ties me here. My job. My friends. I love this goofy little town." Eve stopped, realization dawning. "Wait—you're not worried I'll leave and break his heart. You're worried I'll leave, and he'll go with me."

Mama McT opened her mouth to argue, but then her shoulders slumped. "You could. He could."

"Yeah. We could," Eve agreed. "And I'd hope that your bond with him would be strong enough to withstand that. But did it ever dawn on you that I have spent my whole life longing for what you have? If I'd been welcomed into your family, I'd be crazy to ever leave."

The woman regarded Eve for a moment before admitting softly. "No, I don't suppose it did."

"I am in Callum's life," Eve pushed her plate back and motioned for the check, no longer interested in her breakfast. "I don't know for how long—that's between Callum and me—but I will tell you that I can't imagine my life without him. For his sake, I'd like us to get along. But I'm tired of the eggshells. And the drama. And general shenanigans. The Mama McT I've heard so much about is an amazing woman. I'd like to get to know her."

She didn't wait for the other woman to answer. She paid her check and headed out the door. She had to get on the road if she was going to make her next appointment. But then, when she got back into town, the first thing she was going to do would be to find Callum and have that heart-to-heart they so desperately needed.

It was a little over an hour to Santa Rosa and the adoption event began at 11. She wanted to get there early to have her pick of dogs—and she'd need time to buy all the supplies and everything once she chose her pupper. Eve spent most of her drive, when she wasn't paying attention to the GPS, daydreaming about what kind of dog she'd get. She was hoping for something like Sadie but was open to letting the perfect dog pick her, too.

The rescue group was still setting up when she arrived. She tried not to look too much like a creeper as she hung back, checking out the options from a distance.

"Hey there," an older gentleman greeted her as he walked by with a sign announcing the adoption event. "Are you looking for anything in particular today?"

"I'm hoping to adopt." Eve felt suddenly shy. "I've never had a dog before. But I just got permission from my landlord. And my best friend has a dog—she hooked me up with a good vet and everything."

"That's great." Eve couldn't tell if his smile was patronizing or genuine. She felt like a fool. "Do you know what kind of dog you'd like? Big, small, how active?"

"Um... medium? Not too little. Not giant. I'm pretty open to anything in between. I like to kayak. The dog could go to work with me. But I do work, so it can't be spastic. Is this helping at all?"

The man's smile deepened. "That helps narrow it down a bit, yes. Do you have a preference for male or female? A particular age?"

"I don't care if it's a boy or girl. No puppies. To be honest, I'm kind of hoping the dog will choose me."

"Well, let's weed out the ones that definitely won't work and go from there," he suggested. "Like, that little guy is a pistol. He's going to need lots of room to run."

"I have an apartment. Dog park is nearby, but we should probably skip the 'room to run' crowd."

"Gotcha. This one might be too small for you..."

"He looks like a barker."

"Well, technically they all are, but yeah, he's pretty chatty."

"What about this one?" Eve walked over to a large-ish red dog curled up in the corner of its cage, watching them with sorrowful eyes.

"That's Addelyn."

Eve knelt before the kennel, holding her hand up to the bar to let the dog sniff her, just like Corinne taught her. "Hi, Addelyn. It's nice to meet you."

The dog's tail thumped once in response.

"She can be a bit of a puller on walks, so you'll want a harness for her. She's a helper, that one. Likes to be right in the middle of whatever her foster mom is doing."

"Can I pet her?"

"Yeah, sure. Want me to get her out for you?"

"Yes, please." Eve tried not to get ahead of herself. She admonished herself to be objective. To get to know the dog. Ask questions. Be sure it was the right fit—ten years was a long time to spend with someone you didn't like. But everything in her said this was the one.

Once Addelyn realized she was getting out of the kennel, she came to life. When she wagged her tail, her entire body moved back and forth. Now that the dog was out of the cage, Eve could see that she had a white patch on her chest and white on the very tips of her toes. Her deep brown eyes were lined in what looked like smokey black eyeliner. But mostly, she was just a deep, pretty copper. And when Eve scratched her behind her button ears and asked, "What do you think about maybe coming home with me, Addelyn?" the dog broke into the biggest grin.

"How old is she?" Eve asked.

"She's three. Spayed. Eighty-one pounds—I don't know if your apartment has a weight restriction."

"No, I actually think Moira prefers big dogs. That's my landlord."

"Do you want to take her on a walk? Spend a little time with her?" he offered.

"Yes, absolutely."

"Okay, great. I just need to get some information from you first." He took the dog's leash and handed Eve a clipboard. "For now, I just need that top part. If you decide to apply for her, you can fill out the rest."

It hadn't even occurred to Eve that she might not get the dog she wanted. Suddenly, she was nervous. What if she got attached and then they said no? She scribbled in the pertinent information and then eagerly took the leash back, mentally noting that he hadn't been wrong when he said she was a puller.

Eve could feel her phone vibrating in her back pocket but didn't trust her ability to hang on to the dog and retrieve it, so she let it roll to voicemail. She wondered how long it would take to train Addelyn to walk on a leash as well as Sadie. As they walked, she chattered at the dog, wondering aloud if she liked to play fetch or to play in the water. The dog would periodically stop pulling her along to turn and listen, in those moments seeming to hang on her every word. By the time they'd made their loop and returned to the event, Eve was wholly in love.

"I'd like to fill out the application, please."

"Oh, that's great! Here, I'll trade you again."

Poor Addelyn looked so devastated at being put back in the cage it broke Eve's heart. She wanted to explain to the dog that it was just for a little bit but realized she didn't know that they'd even approve her—or when they'd let her take the dog home if they did.

When she finished filling out the paperwork, she handed the clipboard back. "What's the process from here? How long does it usually take?"

"Well, I'll need to call your vet and your landlord. Once that's verified, you can take her home on a trial basis. We like to do a home visit before paperwork is finalized."

"So, could I possibly take her home today?"

He regarded her for a moment. "Usually, we make the calls and then do the home visit when we bring the dog to you, but I think it would break Addelyn's heart if you left without her today. Do you want to do some shopping while I make the calls?"

"I would love to," she enthused. "What type of food does she like?"

Eve got the must-have list from the man and headed into the

pet store to buy everything Addelyn would need. And, being honest, quite a few things she probably didn't. She sincerely hoped she got approved. If not, Sadie was about to be even more spoiled. Which would be even more unfortunate because Eve picked out the aqua-colored harness specifically because the color would go well with Addelyn.

He had more of a crowd by the time she reemerged, so she knelt by the dog's cage and talked to her, scratching her ears through the bars while they waited.

"Did you get a leash?" he asked before spotting her cart and laughing. "I guess the better question is what didn't you get?"

"I wanted to be sure she had everything she'd need." Eve felt defensive.

"I'm glad to see she'll be so well loved."

Eve brightened, afraid to hope. "Does that mean?"

"Congratulations." He broke into a grin.

"Do you hear that girl? You get to go home with me."

At the volunteer's suggestion, Eve went and unloaded her cart into her trunk while he put the dog's harness on for her. By the time she'd put the cart up and returned, he was waiting with the dog, who could barely contain her exuberance. Eve caught him off guard when she hugged him and thanked him before taking the leash.

She chattered at the dog the whole way home, telling her all about where they'd live and the things they'd do together. She wanted to make a beeline to Callum when she got back in town —she was dying to introduce him to her new friend—but figured the best thing for Addelyn would be to see her new home first. There was already a lot of new happening at once. Eve decided to text him to invite him over for dinner but quickly realized it would have to wait until the dog was settled. She was barely hanging on with two hands and full focus. There was zero chance of her successfully texting and navigating the dog.

But then she realized she couldn't lug everything upstairs with the dog in tow and she wasn't sure she could leave the dog alone just yet. After she walked Addelyn and showed her around the apartment, she decided she'd just leave the dog for one trip and save everything else for when Callum got there, assuming he was willing to come help. The reality was he could have heard about her run-in with his mom and there was every possibility he'd be upset with her over it.

She was saved the phone call when his Jeep pulled in beside her Corolla before she could even fish her phone out of her pocket.

"Callum! Hi! I was just about to call you," she greeted him cheerfully.

His greeting was less cheerful and more yell-y. "Where were you?"

"What? Why?" Eve was startled.

"I've been worried sick about you all day. I heard from half the town that you got into a fight with my mom and then you were just gone. I've been calling and texting and nothing. Are you okay?"

"Yes, I'm okay, and I'm sorry I worried you—but stop yelling at me."

He seemed to deflate with her words, the tension leaving his body now that he was certain she was fine. "I'm Scottish. That's what we do."

"Well, I'm French. We're much more refined than that."

"Nah, darlin'. You're French Creole. I suspect you can hold your own with me."

"But I'm not with you," she reminded him

"Aren't you?" With that, he closed the distance between them and kissed her in a way that left no room for doubt in her mind. Every part of her wanted to melt into him. To stand in the parking lot making out like a couple of teenagers. But then another part of her remembered she had eighty pounds of dog alone in her apartment.

Eve tensed. "Oh no."

"What?" Confusion and concern etched Callum's brow.

"Addelyn. I have to get back upstairs. Come on."

A smarter woman would have grabbed a load of things. Eve was not that woman. She took the stairs two at a time, panicked that either the dog or the apartment would have suffered from her absence.

To her relief, both were fine, although Addelyn broke into one of her enormous grins when she saw Eve. The grin turned into a gruff bark when she saw Callum appear behind her.

"Addelyn, this is Callum. He's a friend."

"Who's this?"

"This is why I wasn't answering my phone all day," Eve explained. "Moira said I could get a dog, so I drove over to an adoption event in Santa Rosa. Between spotty coverage and the excitement and the fact that Addelyn walks me more than I do her right now, I just didn't see your calls. Sorry."

"So, you didn't leave town because my mother chased you off?"

"Would everyone stop acting like I'm going to leave town at the first imposition? Geez."

"I'm sorry, but the thought crossed my mind. Half the town made it sound like World War Three happened at the café."

"You have lived in a small town your entire life. You should know not to believe half of what you hear," she admonished. "I actually think it was the healthiest conversation your mom and I have ever had. It's fine."

"Yeah?"

"Yeah."

"So, what about the part everyone told me about you telling my mom that you can't imagine your life without me? Can I believe that?"

Eve put her arms around his waist, pulling him to her as she said, "Yeah, that part they got right."

"Good. Because I can't imagine my life without you, either." He bent his head to kiss her.

She pulled back a bit and eyed him. "We still have some things to talk about. Stuff to sort out."

"Of course."

"And you need to unload my car."

"Naturally."

"It's super full. It's possible I bought too many dog toys and beds. And dishes."

"So, the woman who came to town with no furniture now has an abundance of dog furniture?" he clarified.

"Something like that. Oh, that reminds me. I still need to do something nice for you."

"Why's that?"

"I know you were the original furniture fairy. I found a way to repay everyone else's kindness. You're the last one on my list."

"Eve, don't you get it?"

"What?"

"You. You're all I need. Say you'll stay in my arms, and we'll call it square."

"That, I can do." This time, she kissed him in such a way that left no room for doubt. "Just as soon as you unload my car. Oh, and buy my dinner. Your mom interrupted my breakfast, so you kind of owe me."

"Uh-huh."

They wound up unloading the car together before walking the dog down to their favorite Thai place to pick up some takeout. Callum manned the leash since Addelyn had a tougher time dragging him. The couple held hands as they moseyed down the street. More than one person called out a hello to them as they passed. Eve realized she knew their names. She knew their stories, and they knew hers. For the first time in her life, she belonged.

The End

ABOUT THE AUTHOR

Heather Huffman is a multi-genre author with publications in contemporary romance, romantic suspense, women's fiction, and even a new cozy mystery line launching summer 2021. Quirky, optimistic, and a bit of a wanderer, Huffman cares deeply about causes pertaining to social justice and women's issues and has spent the past decade working with various charities that fight poverty, empower women, and fight human trafficking. At the center of her world are her three grown sons, her Australian Shepherd, and a possibly spoiled puppy she shares entirely too many pictures of. Learn more at heatherhuffman.net.

ALSO BY HEATHER HUFFMAN

If you liked meeting Nora, you won't want to miss out on her adventures in St. Augustine!

BODY IN THE BOOKS

Sometimes, owning a bookstore can be murder.

When Nora Jones inherits a dusty old bookshop from her estranged uncle, she moves to St. Augustine to tie up loose ends and maybe learn a bit about the man she never knew.

Only what first appeared to be a heart attack turns out to be murder, and there's no shortage of suspects. The detective assigned to the case might be handsome and charming, but Nora's convinced he's chasing down the wrong lead.

With her newly-inherited Greyhound named Margo and a quirky band of friends in tow, Nora decides to track down the killer. She finds herself in a race to solve the murder before she becomes the next body in the books.

Body in the Books is the first installment of the Nora Jones cozy mystery series. You won't want to miss this humorous whodunit that's being likened to Scooby Doo for grownups.

Available July 13, 2021. Preorder at Amazon today!

And if liked Wes Dryden, you won't want to miss the story of him and the woman he was dating "in Kansas or Oklahoma or something."

ELUSIVE MAGIC

Some might call it a midlife crisis, but Josie Novak prefers to think of it as a midlife awakening.

With her relationship in shambles and her career floundering, Josie is at a crossroads.

Enter fairy godmother aka best friend Brigitte, offering Josie a chance to make the dream of opening her own bar a reality. But achieving dreams is not an easy thing, especially when you're dating over forty and helping friends through the highs and lows of marriages, babies being born and babies leaving home, and all the other things life throws at this group of women as they navigate modern-day femininity.

Both heart-wrenchingly sad and laugh-out-loud funny, this fortysomething coming of age story teaches Josie that being a woman might not be a fairy tale, but it is an elusive magic all its own.

Buy *Elusive Magic* at your favorite online retailer, and keep an eye out for Everyday Magic, available August 2021.

Billionaires, castaways, and second chances. The books that started it all are full of action, adventure, romance, suspense—and always hope, love, and laughter.

THE THROWAWAYS

Surprisingly warm and funny, *The Throwaways* are twelve novels that don't shy away from the dark corners of this world but always shine the light of hope. At the core of the series is a group of strong but often unlikely heroes and heroines coming from all walks of life whose lives intertwine as they fight for justice, for love, and to leave their indelible mark on this world.

Immerse yourself in a world of suspense, laughter, and love with *The Throwaways*.

Now available at Amazon, or read for free with your Kindle Unlimited Subscription.

Made in the USA
Monee, IL
19 November 2021